THE REPORT CARD

Andrew Clements

SIMON & SCHUSTER BOOKS FOR YOUNG READERS
New York   London   Toronto   Sydney

for my son,
John Edward Clements

Thanks
to Harrison Collins for giving me my first job as a teacher;
to Alfie Kohn for his book *The Schools Our Children Deserve*;
to Charles P. Pierce for his *Boston Globe Magazine* article "Testing Times";
and to Howard Gardner for his work to establish a broader definition of intelligence.

SIMON & SCHUSTER BOOKS FOR YOUNG READERS
An imprint of Simon & Schuster Children's Publishing Division
1230 Avenue of the Americas, New York, New York 10020

Book design by O'Lanso Gabbidon

The text for this book is set in Meridien.
Manufactured in the United States of America
10 9 8 7 6 5 4 3 2 1

Library of Congress Cataloging-in-Publication Data
Clements, Andrew.
The report card / Andrew Clements.
p. cm.
Summary: Fifth grader Nora Rowley has always hidden the fact that she is a genius from everyone because all she wants is to be normal, but when she comes up with a plan to prove that grades are not important, things begin to get out of control.
ISBN 0-689-84515-4
[1. Grading and marking (Students)—Fiction. 2. Achievement tests—Fiction. 3. Schools—Fiction. 4. Genius—Fiction. 5. Friendship—Fiction.] I. Title.
PZ7.C59118 Re 2004
[Fic]—dc21
2003007384

FIRST
EDITION

one

BAD GRADES

There were only about fifteen kids on the late bus because it was Friday afternoon. I sat near the back with Stephen, and he kept pestering me.

"Come on, Nora. I showed you my report card. I want to see if I beat you in math. Let me see what you got. Come on."

"No," I said. "No means no. I'm not opening it. I had to go to school every day, and I had to sit there and take the tests and quizzes when they told me to. But I have a choice about when I look at my grades, and right now I choose not to. So ask me on Monday."

Stephen is my best friend, but I'm not sure he would have admitted it. If any of his buddies had been on the bus, he wouldn't have been sitting anywhere near me. In fifth grade a guy's best friend isn't supposed to be a girl—which is one of the most immature ideas in the universe. Your best friend is the person you care about the most and who cares back just as much. And that's the way it was with me and Stephen. It wasn't a girl-boy thing. It was just a fact.

Stephen was persistent. He'd been having a hard time with his schoolwork for the past ten weeks, and he was obsessed with grades. So he wouldn't shut up about my report card. On and on and on. And our bus ride home took twenty minutes. "Come on, Nora. It's not fair. You know what I got, but I don't know what you got. I wanna see your grades. C'mon, lemme see 'em."

Another fact: Sometimes no doesn't mean no forever. There was only about a block to go before our bus stop, but I couldn't stand Stephen's whining another second. Besides, the truth is, I was dying to know my spelling grade. I was sure about my grades in all the other subjects, but I thought I might have messed up in spelling. So I pulled my report card out of my backpack and slapped it into Stephen's hands. I didn't even care that my whole name was printed right on the label: Nora Rose Rowley.

"Here," I said. "This is your prize for being the most annoying person in the world."

Stephen said, "All riiight!" and he had those grades out of the envelope in about three seconds.

Stephen's face went blank and his mouth dropped open. And it was like he couldn't talk. Or breathe. He finally spluttered and said, "No *way*, Nora! This *can't* be right! Mrs. Noyes . . . and Mrs. Zhang . . . and *everybody*! These are the wrong grades!"

I ignored his amazement. I said, "Just tell me what I got in spelling, okay?"

Stephen's eyes flickered down the page and then he said, "You . . . you got a C."

"*Rats!*" and I kicked the seat in front of us. "I *knew* it! A lousy C—how could I be so *stupid*!"

Stephen was wishing he hadn't begged to see my grades, and his face showed it. He gulped and said, "Um . . . Nora? I hate to tell you, but all your other grades are . . ."

I cut him off. "I know what they are."

Stephen was completely confused. He said, "But . . . but if you know what the others are, then why are you mad about the C in spelling? Because all the others are . . . *Ds*! You got a D in *everything*! All Ds—except for that one C."

"*Rats*!" I said again. "*Spelling*!"

Stephen struggled on. "But . . . but spelling is your *best* grade," and to reassure himself he said, ". . . because a C is *better* than a D, right?"

I shook my head, and then I said more than I should have. "Not always," I said. "C is *not* better if you're trying to get a D."

That *really* confused Stephen. And I didn't want him to have time to think about it. I grabbed my report card back and said, "So what did you get in spelling?"

I knew the answer to that question because I'd already seen Stephen's report card. Plus, spelling is always his best subject.

Stephen said, "I . . . I got an A."

"And is that the grade you were trying to get?"

He squinted and then said, "Um . . . yeah, I guess so."

"Then you got what you were trying for, and that's good. That's a good grade, Stephen."

He said, "Um . . . thanks."

We got off the bus at the corner and started walking along the street toward our houses. Stephen didn't say another word.

I could tell he was worried about my grades. And that was just like him—to be worried about someone other than himself. Which is why it was a good thing that Stephen had someone like me looking out for him.

Because I had gotten those Ds on purpose. I had meant to get *all* Ds. And those Ds were probably going to get me into big trouble.

But I didn't care about that.

I had gotten those Ds for Stephen.

two

THE FACTS OF ME

My room was "a mess." I was supposed to "get it all straightened up" before dinner. "Or else." Mom's orders.

But I wasn't in the mood to clean. Or scared enough. So I just lay there on my bed, thinking. Which wasn't unusual. And the thought came very clearly that a messy room was the least of my problems. That was a fact.

I've always loved facts. That's because facts don't change. And I think that's why I sometimes hate facts too.

I've been discovering facts about myself for a long time. It's like I've been doing experiments for years so I can figure out what makes me me—the facts of me.

Here's one fact I've discovered: I have the opposite of amnesia. I don't think I've ever forgotten anything. I can remember all the way back. I can remember the smell of the soft, blue cloth my mom tucked under my chin to catch the drips when I drank baby formula from a bottle. I can remember each red polka dot on the hat of the stuffed clown puppet I slept with in my crib—twelve dots. I can remember the yellow-and-white diamond pattern on the plastic liner of my playpen and the taste of those biscuits I chewed on before my teeth popped through my gums. I remember all that stuff.

And lying there on my bed, I remembered back to when I thought everyone else was just like me. Because that's the way it seemed to me in the beginning. I couldn't tell the difference between myself and everybody else. I thought everyone else was thinking and feeling and seeing the same things I was. But that was not a fact.

There—the way I was thinking just there? That's another fact about me. I do that constantly, that kind of analyzing. I've always been like that.

Then my mind went racing through its filing system, and I remembered every detail of the day when I first started to see I was different.

It happened because of my big sister, Ann.

She was six years older, so it was like we lived on different planets. Whenever we got anywhere near each other, Ann's planet usually crushed my planet.

It was a Saturday morning right after I had learned how to walk, and Ann dumped a big, five-hundred-piece jigsaw puzzle onto the floor in our family room. The picture on the box showed a scene from a Muppets movie.

Ann thought she was this huge puzzle expert, and when I went over to watch, she said, "No, Nora. This isn't a *baby* puzzle. Get away!"

I moved back a little, but I kept watching. I've never been scared of Ann. That's because I've always understood her. All Ann has ever wanted is for everybody to beg her to be the queen of the universe.

First Ann turned all the pieces picture-side up, and then she picked out all the pieces with straight edges. Those were the frame pieces because Ann always puts the frame of a puzzle together first.

After the frame was done, Ann started looking for a part of Miss Piggy's ear. So I leaned forward and put my pointer finger on a puzzle piece.

"Hey!" said Ann, and she pushed my hand away. Then she saw. I had pointed to the piece she was looking for. She picked it up, turned it around, and pushed it into place. Narrowing her eyes at me, Ann said, "Where's the one that goes here?" and she put her finger on a piece at the bottom edge of the frame.

So I pointed again and that piece fit too.

"And the next one?" asked Ann.

Again I pointed and again it fit. Because it wasn't hard for me. I could see all the pieces at once and I could see exactly where each of them went. They were right there, plain as day.

Then Ann got an idea, and it wasn't a very nice one. Reaching toward a part of the puzzle that was all Kermit-green, she put her finger on one piece and said, "What goes . . . here?"

I ran my eyes over all those puzzle pieces scattered next to the frame. There must have been a hundred that were mostly green. Ann thought I was stumped. But I wasn't. I reached out and picked up one piece and gave it to her.

Ann said, "Nice try, Nora. At least you got a green one. Like I said, this is not a *baby* puzzle.

So go away." Then Ann looked at the piece in her hand and the part of the frame she still had her finger on. She turned my piece around once and brought it closer to the frame. It was the right piece.

"How did you do that?" asked Ann. Now she was more curious than jealous.

But I just looked at all the pieces and picked up another one. And Ann put it in the puzzle, hooking it on to the other piece I had found.

Then Ann said, "Here, Nora. You put some pieces in the puzzle. You just have to push each one down, like this, with your thumb. Start right here."

I could feel how Ann was watching me. She had never looked at me that way before. I didn't know I was doing anything unusual—because for me, the puzzle was so easy. I didn't have to look and look and try out ten pieces to find a right one. I could just see the next piece. I didn't have to slow down and I didn't make any mistakes.

Ann ran and got Mom. Then I felt two pairs of eyes staring at me. So I stopped.

"Go on, keep doing the puzzle, Nora," said

Ann. "Show Mommy. Find the piece for right there."

Then Mom said, "Go on, honey. Help Ann do the puzzle. Go on."

It felt like they were pushing me with their eyes. They wanted a performance. But I was just being me.

So I did nothing.

Ann said, "Come *on*, Nora. Just one piece. Come *on*," and she grabbed my hand and pulled it toward the unmatched pieces.

I yelled, "*No!*" and I yanked my hand away. That was it for me. Puzzle playtime was over.

But later, when I was supposed to be taking a nap, I climbed out of my crib and crawled backward down the stairs. I went into the family room and sat down on the floor and put the whole puzzle together. I took a long look at Miss Piggy and Kermit and Fozzie Bear and Animal, and then I took the puzzle apart and left everything just the way it had been. And then I took my nap.

That day I learned some important facts about me. I learned that what seemed normal to me seemed strange to other people. I also learned that I didn't like to perform. And that I hated to be pushed around.

For a week or so after that, I could tell my mom and Ann kept watching me. And my dad and my big brother, too. They were all watching to see if I would do anything else that was smart or clever. So I was careful, which might seem weird, but it was a fact. If my mom or dad or Ann or my big brother or any of the kids at day care started looking at me funny, I would stop whatever I was doing. I didn't want to be stared at. So I was careful.

And a few months later, when I figured out how to read, I was careful about that, too. Reading was amazing and wonderful and exciting, but I didn't tell anybody. And there were reasons. My brother's name is Todd, and he's three years older than I am, there in between me and Ann. When I first started reading, Todd was in kindergarten, and he didn't know how to read at all. So I figured that if little baby Nora let anyone see she could read, it would be a big deal. And I thought it might also make Todd feel bad, or mad at me, or both. Plus, I didn't want my mom and dad to make me read my own stories at bedtime. So I kept the fact of my reading a secret.

I was still lying on my bed, thinking and thinking. And then I remembered my report card—the Ds on my first report card of fifth grade. Those Ds had become a fact. It had been nice to forget about them for a few minutes. But forgetting about a fact does not make the fact go away.

And I knew that pretty soon my mom was going to yell that it was dinnertime.

I got up off my bed, walked over to my desk, grabbed my report card, and licked the flap of the envelope. The glue tasted terrible. I waited a second and then pressed the flap shut. Now the report card was hidden away, sealed inside its ugly, brown, recycled-paper envelope. And I even flattened out the little tabs of the brass fastener.

Then I instantly analyzed what I'd done, and I knew why I had sealed the envelope. Those Ds were like a time bomb—tick, tick, tick, BOOM! The explosion was inevitable. I was putting it off until the last possible second.

I had thought about getting those Ds for a

long time. I felt pretty sure that my plan made sense—but still, my mom and dad had always been crazy about grades.

And I had to face a fact: Those Ds were going to have to be explained.

But not the part about Stephen. About how those Ds were related to him.

The part about Stephen wouldn't have to be explained until much later.

Maybe never.

three

SCHOOL AND STEPHEN

Soon my mom was going to call me down-stairs for dinner. And after dinner would come The Reading of the Grades. And then, BOOM!

My whole life was flashing in front of me like a report on the six o'clock news. Memories kept flooding in. I couldn't help it. And I realized that this explosion had been building up ever since I first went to school.

Another fact from the memory files: I had gotten off to a bad start in kindergarten.

That's mostly because I spent my first two weeks at Philbrook Elementary School hiding under a table in Mrs. Bridge's room, pretending I was a cat. I meowed and hissed, and at snack time I poured my milk into a plastic bowl I had brought from home. That was so I could lap up the milk with my tongue.

I acted like a cat until 11:53 every day. Then I would get up, dust off my knees, put on my jacket, and get ready to ride the bus to my afternoon day care.

The cat business had started a month before kindergarten began. I had read this great article in *National Geographic* about leopards, and then I had learned everything else I could about cats. And I had decided that cats were amazing and wonderful, and I thought it would be fun to see what it felt like to be a cat. That's where the idea came from.

But the real reason I began being a cat at school was because I knew that if I started doing schoolwork in kindergarten, it would be too easy. Everyone would have thought I was too good at it. Being too good would have made me seem too different. It was so much easier to be different by being a cat.

No one would suspect that a cat liked to read the *Encyclopaedia Britannica*. No one would guess that a cat had memorized thirty-eight of the poems in *A Child's Garden of Verses*.

No one would suspect that a cat had taught herself to understand Spanish by watching the Univision channel. And no one would suspect that a cat was interested in maps and history and archaeology and astronomy and space travel and the Latin names for animals—like *Felis catus*, the domestic cat.

I was smart, but I didn't have much experience. I was still a five-year-old kid. So I made a miscalculation. Because I thought that once everyone at school had gotten used to the idea that I was pretending to be a cat, they'd pretty much leave me alone.

But, of course, that wasn't the way it worked at school.

Right away Mrs. Bridge called my mom. My mom got upset, and then she told my dad and he got upset.

I've always loved my mom and dad, but they tend to get excited too easily, especially about school stuff. That was why I always kept one part of myself hidden from them—the smart part. So back when I was in kindergarten, my parents didn't even know I could read. And really, it hadn't been that hard for me to keep my smart part a secret. My mom was working for a real estate company and my dad was running his own business, and then there was the housework and the yard work plus three kids to take care of. Fact: My mom and dad have always been busier than sparrows. I never tried to get attention and I didn't cause any problems, so everyone left me alone most of the time. I was careful never to give my mom and dad anything to worry about. I spent a lot of time looking at books when I was little, and I'm sure they noticed that. But they must have thought I just liked to look at the pictures. And I also spent a lot of time watching TV.

But it's not like I was some kind of weirdo zombie tubehead hermit bookworm, because that would have *really* made them worry. I had friends at day care and in the neighborhood. And I liked to play soccer and mess around outside. Mom and Dad had thought I was an ordinary kid.

Then I went to school and turned into KinderKat.

So my mom and dad got worried and they called the principal, Mrs. Hackney. And then the special education teacher and the guidance counselor got involved, and everyone at school decided I had a learning disability. I could feel how they all started looking at me, and I didn't like that. I didn't want people to think there was something wrong with me. So after two weeks I knew I had to stop being a cat.

But I didn't want to start being myself. That seemed dangerous too.

I thought about it and the idea I got was so simple: *Don't be a cat; be a copycat!* I decided that every day I would be like a different kid in my class. I would become a living average of all the other children in my kindergarten.

So one Wednesday morning, instead of getting down under the table, I picked out one kid to copy. I started doing whatever Stephen Curtis was doing—not exactly but pretty close. And he had no idea I was copying him.

When Stephen sat on a rug square and watched Susan help Mrs. Bridge pick out the right day of the week to hang on the date board, I sat and watched too.

When Stephen got out a puzzle, so did I, and I took as long to do my puzzle as it took Stephen to do his.

When Stephen began playing with blocks, so did I, and I tried to make my building look sort of like Stephen's.

When Stephen sat at a table and tried to draw the letter *A* with a pencil, I sat down nearby and worked on the letter *B* with a crayon. I could have written any letter perfectly, and hundreds of whole words, too. But I made it look like writing a *B* was as hard for me as writing that *A* was for Stephen.

The morning went by quickly, and I was amazed at how many different things Stephen did. Kindergarten took on a new meaning for me. It had become my laboratory.

The next day I decided to be like Caitlyn. She threaded beads, and so did I. She played in the dress-up corner, and so did I. When Caitlyn colored some butterflies, I did too, and I even joined Caitlyn and three other girls in a game of tag during outside recess. It was another educational day for me.

Mrs. Bridge was thrilled about the sudden change in my behavior, and so was the special education teacher, and, of course, so were my parents. And once I turned into an average kid, the pressure stopped.

However, I was just getting started with my research. Helen, Laura, Ron, Kathy, Philip,

Jeremy, Karen, James, Kim, Susan, Elliot—I played copycat day after day, always shadowing a different kid. Each day was new and interesting. I felt like I was part of the class, and I liked that feeling.

But I also learned that I liked being so smart. Because by kindergarten I had figured out an important fact about me: I was a genius. The things that most kids found difficult were easy for me. I had seen the other children working hard to learn their letter shapes, working hard to understand the sounds each letter made, working hard just to make their fingers hold a pencil or a pair of scissors. I knew that none of them were thinking the way I was, or reading the kinds of things I could read. Megan was the only other kid in my class who could read at all, and just some simple picture books.

Day by day I got a clearer idea of how far ahead I was. That didn't make me think I was better than the other kids, though. The more I got to know them, the more I admired them. I was amazed by all their hard work. I realized that I didn't have to work like they did and that I never had. School was different for me. Everything was different for me.

There were fifteen kids in my kindergarten, and each one got a turn being copied. So it was about two weeks before I spent another day copying Stephen. And it was wonderful because right away I could tell he had made some progress. Stephen must have been working on his letter shapes because now he could draw *A* through O perfectly. Except he made his capital *G* backward every time. I wished I could help Stephen with that, but I knew I didn't dare. Not if I wanted to keep my secret. So I chose *D* as my backward letter, and I thought, *In a couple weeks, when it's time to copy Stephen again, maybe he'll have that* G *turned around.*

But two weeks seemed too long to wait.

That's why I followed Stephen the very next day, and then the next three days after that. And then all the next week, too. I watched everything Stephen did for nine days in a row, and I heard everything he said. It was an in-depth study.

Stephen wasn't one of the smartest kids in

the class. I could see that. But Stephen was such a good worker. If he couldn't do something, he was patient and he didn't give up. If something was too hard, Stephen didn't get mad at himself. He simply moved on and then went back to it. And sooner or later he figured it out. He liked to sit alone sometimes and look out the window or draw shapes with a pencil or a crayon. He didn't *look* at the pictures in the picture books; he studied them. Also, when Stephen played a game, he always played fair. And the most important thing to me was that during all the time I watched him, Stephen never said or did one mean or angry thing. Not once. To anyone—even if someone was mean to him first.

Then one Monday morning Stephen was absent. Same thing on Tuesday and Wednesday. I almost called his house Wednesday night to make sure he wasn't dying or something. Because the thought of school without Stephen was suddenly the worst thing I could imagine. When he got off his bus on Thursday morning, I wanted to run over and give him a big hug. Of course, I didn't.

But that's when I decided that Stephen was going to be my best friend. He was just so nice. Because I thought, *Who could be a better friend than Stephen?* And I also thought, *If Stephen was my friend, then I could help him.* Because that's what friends do.

The best thing that happened during my first year at Philbrook Elementary School was getting to be friends with Stephen Curtis. And the best thing that happened during third grade was when Stephen's family moved to a house down the street from me. And the best thing that's happened all five years I've known Stephen is that we've kept getting put into the same classrooms with the same teachers.

So I stayed best friends with Stephen. And I kept helping him. Carefully. Not show-offy. Not smarty-pantsy. Just some friendly help once in a while. With little things. I was like an extra teacher. Half the time Stephen didn't even know he needed help or that I was giving it.

It was during fourth grade. That's when Stephen started to change. It was after the big tests we all had to take at the beginning of fourth grade, the Connecticut Mastery Testing. Because Stephen didn't get good scores. And I knew why. I had watched him making faces and chewing his pencil and looking up at the clock every other minute during the tests. It was the pressure that got him, even after all the hours and hours and hours we had spent in class getting ready for the tests. I mean, he probably wouldn't have done that great even without the pressure—because, like I said, as far as school work went, he was an average student. But all the time pressure didn't help, that's for sure. So Stephen's scores on the CMT were sort of low. Not terrible, just low.

My scores weren't great either. That's because I found all this information about the tests on the Internet. I figured out how many questions I had to miss on each section so it would look like I was an average student. My parents weren't happy with my scores, but what could they do? In first, second, and third grades I had always been an average student, and that's all there was to it—and now the big tests proved it.

So I didn't care about my CMT scores at all. But for some reason, Stephen did. He cared about his scores a lot. And from what he said, I guess his parents made a big deal about his test scores too.

I noticed a change in Stephen right away. He got mad at himself if he messed up on assignments or tests. He worried about tests and quizzes—spelling tests, too, and he was good at spelling. He even started pretending he was sick sometimes so he could stay home from school. And Stephen had never used to do that. The worst part was that he didn't seem as happy.

Our fourth-grade teacher was Mrs. Rosen and she was great. She said the test scores didn't mean anything. She called them a snapshot, just a chance to look and see where we needed to improve. She said not to worry if the scores seemed low because there was plenty of time to improve. I understood her. And all of that was true. But I could tell Stephen didn't believe Mrs. Rosen. He felt like he wasn't good at school anymore. He felt like school was a struggle.

And Stephen wasn't the only one. All the kids started keeping track of test scores and homework grades. School was suddenly all about the competition, and grades were how you could tell the winners from the losers. Every assignment and quiz became a contest. I even saw a couple of kids cheating on a spelling test.

Then in the middle of fourth grade, three kids from our class were chosen to be in the Gifted and Talented Program. The gifted kids went to special classes. They read special books. They had a special teacher, and if they worked hard, they were moved ahead. They could even skip grades. It felt like school had turned into a big race, and it looked like the gifted kids had already won.

Which was one more reason that everyone in our class started sorting themselves out into the smart kids and the average kids and the dumb kids. And that was terrible because Stephen started thinking he was one of the dumb kids. It wasn't true, not at all, not for any of the kids. But that's how Stephen felt.

Fourth grade was a miserable year for Stephen. And for me, too—because a person can't be happy if her best friend isn't.

Stephen was glad when fourth grade ended.

It felt like his troubles were over, and summer was going to be great, just like always.

But I was looking ahead to fifth grade. Stephen didn't know what was coming in fifth grade. He only had one little brother, so Stephen was the first kid in his family to go through the schools in Philbrook, Connecticut.

Not me. I knew about fifth grade in Philbrook. I had watched Ann go through fifth grade and then Todd. Fifth grade was when Ann had started turning into a grim little A-making machine—with plenty of pushing from Mom and Dad. Fifth-grade grades were real letter grades, just like the junior high and the high school—no more cute plusses and checks and minuses. Fifth-grade grades were the real thing: As and Bs and Cs and Ds and Fs. Fifth-grade grades would be used to see which kids got into the higher math classes at the junior high. Fifth-grade grades would be used to see which kids got into the advanced English classes and the foreign language program and the accelerated science classes. In Philbrook, Connecticut, fifth-grade grades mattered.

And if Stephen got messed up by the Mastery

Testing and a little competition during fourth grade, then fifth grade was going to feel about ten times worse. When Stephen hit fifth grade, it was going to be like a train wreck.

During this first grading term I had seen it already starting to happen. It could only get worse.

Unless someone thought up a way to help.

And that was my job. Because that's what a best friend does. If she can, she helps.

And that's what I was thinking about when my mom yelled, "Dinnertime!"

"And don't forget," she called upstairs to Ann, Todd, and me. "Please bring your report cards to the table."

four

THE READING OF THE GRADES

My mom had made a fantastic meal and we ate in the dining room. Steak and baked potatoes and green beans and a fresh fruit salad and hot rolls and butter and strawberry jelly. There was a white tablecloth and lace placemats and tall green candles and the best silverware. Even cloth napkins.

We always had great food on report card day. No meatloaf. No macaroni and cheese. No tuna-noodle casserole. Not on report card day.

Then came dessert, also wonderful. Apple crisp made with fresh apples from the orchard over on Route 27. Plus vanilla ice cream.

But I wasn't that hungry. It reminded me of the last meal they serve to a prisoner before an execution.

After the dessert dishes were cleared away, we were all sitting at the table, and my mom said, "All right, who wants to be first to read a report card tonight?"

It was a pointless question. The Reading of the Grades was a well-established ritual. It followed a definite pattern. Ann always read her grades first, then Todd, and then me.

Ann said, "I'll go first." No smile. Ann was all business.

It was Ann's junior year in high school. Ann is tall, blond, athletic, and intense. Kind of pretty, too. People say I look like her, except I'm not tall. And my hair's more reddish than blond. And I try not to be intense. So I guess those people who say we look alike are crazy.

Ann had been elected junior-class president. She was cocaptain of the girl's field hockey team and the girls' basketball team. She had been the youngest member of last year's Math Decathlon, and the team had placed first in the state competition. Ann was taking four Advanced Placement courses and one honors class. She was trying to graduate from high school a semester early. She wanted to get a scholarship to Georgetown University and study international relations. Intense is the right word.

Mom smiled and said, "All right, Ann. Let's hear how you did."

Ann unfolded her computer-printed grade sheet. I knew what was coming. Everyone knew what was coming.

Ann began reading. "Honors Chemistry, A plus. A.P. English, A. A.P. World History, A. A.P. Physics, A plus. A.P. Spanish, A. Phys Ed, A plus. Mixed Chorus, A plus. And an A minus in Driver's Education, but that won't count in my class rank."

"That's terrific, Annie!" My dad's smile made him look like a piano. He said, "Not much room for improvement, and that's the way it ought to be. Great! Just *great*!"

Mom said, "You should be very proud of yourself, Ann. All your hard work is really paying off." Then turning to my side of the table, Mom said, "Okay, who's next—Nora or Todd?"

Another pointless question. Never in his life had Todd let me do anything ahead of him. He said, "I'm next."

Todd was in eighth grade. He had lots of friends and lots of interests, like mountain biking and snowboarding and playing electric guitar and being a 1960s rock-and-roll trivia nut. Todd's school sport was soccer, but he wasn't a star player—which is what I am. And that's not bragging about my soccer playing. That's just a fact. Schoolwork wasn't easy for Todd, especially reading. But Mom and Dad kept after him, so he worked pretty hard, and his grades usually showed it.

Todd cleared his throat, glanced at Dad and then at Mom, gulped once, pushed his straight, brown hair up off his forehead, and then began to read. Todd always read his best grades first. "Gym class, A plus. Math, A minus. Science, B . . . uh, no, I mean it's a B *plus*. Social Studies, B. And a B minus in English . . . but I was only two points away from a plain B."

Mom and Dad nodded thoughtfully for a moment, and then Mom said, "Well, that's a pretty good report, Todd. But I don't think it's really the *best* you can do, is it? Especially that B minus in English. I'd think you'd be a little disappointed with that. At the conference last month Mrs. Flood said you need to spend more time with your writing, and you need to take your outside reading assignments more seriously. Don't you think that would help?"

Todd nodded and said, "Yeah, I guess. But

still, Mom, I got a B average and that's good. You should see Tom's grades."

"But we're not talking about Tom." Dad was not smiling. "We're talking about you. You're almost in high school now, and you've got to start being more serious. Grades like that might get you into a state school, or into a little college somewhere out in the middle of nowhere. But those grades wouldn't get you into a good college. No way. Time to get down to business. Agreed?"

Todd made a sheepish face and nodded. "Yeah. Okay. I'll . . . I'll do better. I will."

And then all eyes swung to me.

My cheeks felt hot. I hadn't planned well for this part. I had thought reading my grades out loud wouldn't be a problem. But it was.

Before Mom could ask, I said, "I don't want to read them. Don't try to tell me that my fifth-grade grades are important, because I know for a fact that they aren't. And they're all based on a bunch of stupid information that anybody with half a brain can memorize. Tests and grades and all of it—it's all . . . just stupid."

Shocked silence.

Then in a calm voice my dad said, "Please read your grades to us, Nora."

I shook my head. "You can look at them if you want to. But *I'm* not going to read them. My grades are *my* business, and nobody else's."

My dad started to say something, but Mom cut in and said, "Nora, I know this may be hard for you, but it's important. You're in fifth grade now. You have to get used to the fact that grades *do* matter. They matter a lot. So please, read your grades. We know everybody's different, and not everyone's going to do as well as everyone else. We're not comparing you to Todd or Ann or anybody. We just want to be able to talk about school and how you're doing, talk about it as a family."

I didn't budge. "There's nothing to talk about. May I please be excused?"

That was too much for my dad. "No!" he shouted. "You may *not* be excused! You're not leaving this table until you have read your grades out loud to your family!"

I put my sealed report card on the middle of my placemat. "Fine," I said. "Sit here as long as you like. But I'm *not* reading my grades."

A long three minutes passed in silence. Then I folded my arms and put my head down on the table.

Todd cleared his throat and said, "Dad, Tommy's mom is gonna be here in ten minutes. She's driving us to the movies and I've got to get ready. So may I be excused? *Please?* And could I have my allowance?"

Five minutes after that I was alone at the table.

Around nine-thirty I pulled three chairs together so I could lie down. I kicked my shoes off, moved a bunch of things out of the way, and slid the tablecloth toward me so I could use it like a blanket.

I'd been asleep, so I'm not sure what time it was. But it was later and I heard my mom say, "Carry her up to bed, Jim. She's won this round, and we might as well admit it."

I kept my eyes shut.

My dad said, "Yup. She can be a tough little cookie, all right. She'd make a great lawyer, I bet. Except first she'd have to get into law school somewhere."

I heard the sound of ripping paper. And I

knew what it was. He was opening my report card.

I heard him pull in a sharp breath, and then, "My *gosh*! No wonder Nora wouldn't read this! Look, Carla—all *Ds*! Everything but spelling, and that's a C!"

"Goodness!" That was Mom. "I don't *believe* it! How did this happen?"

Dad said, "Well, let's shake her and sit her up right here and find out!"

Mom said, "No, Jim, not now. Poor child—think how ashamed she must feel about such terrible marks. Just take her upstairs. We can talk about it tomorrow."

I felt the tablecloth slip off my back and legs, and then Dad's strong arms lifted me up.

It had been a long time since my dad had carried me up to bed.

I heard my mom behind us on the stairs. "Careful you don't bang her head on anything."

And my dad said softly, "With grades like those, it prob'ly couldn't hurt."

Mom said, "That's not funny."

I was glad they didn't try to get me into my

pajamas because I'm sure it would have tickled. My mom just peeled off my socks, tucked the quilt up under my chin, kissed me softly on the forehead, and then closed my door.

I opened my eyes and stared into the darkness.

I wondered if I had done enough thinking about my plan. Because first I had tried to think about what I wanted to accomplish, and then I had tried to think of all the steps I had to take, and how my steps would lead to the steps other people would take. I had done a lot of thinking, and that's something I've gotten good at.

But had I thought of every single thing that could go wrong at every single step, and had I thought of enough ways to get around each possible problem?

Lying there in the dark, I faced a fact: I wouldn't know if my plan would work until it did. Or didn't.

five

SOLITARY CONFINEMENT

Ann and Todd were still in bed when I walked into the kitchen on Saturday morning. My parents were sitting at the table with their coffee mugs. I could tell they had been waiting for me.

I didn't like this part of the plan. This part of the plan was going to be pretty hard on Mom and Dad. And so were some other parts. It wasn't really fair to them, but it couldn't be helped. After all, I wasn't the one who had made up the rules around here.

Mom didn't even say "good morning." She said, "We opened your grade report last night, Nora."

My dad shook his head and growled, "Never seen such bad grades in my life—even on *my* report cards."

I said, "I don't want to talk about it. You saw the grades. I got Ds. And one C. Those are my grades. I don't want to talk about it."

"Nora, please," Mom said. "There must be a reason you got such awful grades. Are you unhappy? Have the children at school been teasing you? Have you been feeling sick? Or is it something else?"

I shook my head as I scanned the row of cereal boxes on the counter. I poured some cornflakes into a bowl and said, "I don't want to talk about it, Mom. I got the grades I got, and that's all there is to it."

Dad exploded. "'*All there is to it*'?! Well, then you're grounded, young lady! And *that's* all there is to it! You don't want to spill the beans and let us help you out, then that's the way it is. You can just sit in your room until you decide to cooperate."

I munched my cereal, swallowed, and took a sip of orange juice. I said, "Fine by me." Then I said, "Am I allowed to read, or do I have to sit in the corner and look at the flowers on the wallpaper?" Which was a lot sassier than usual. But that was part of the plan too.

Mom put a hand on Dad's arm. She said, "Nora, don't be disrespectful. You know better than that. And you know us better than that too. We only want to help you. But first you've got to help us."

I looked at them. "But I don't want any help. Did I ask you to come to school and take my tests for me? Did I ask you to read my assignments for me? Or do my homework? I don't need help."

They didn't talk any more and neither did I. After my last spoonful of cereal, I tipped up my bowl and drank the milk. I wiped the milk off my upper lip, laid my napkin on the table, got up, and put my bowl and spoon and glass into the dishwasher. Then I said, "I'll be up in my room."

I spent the rest of Saturday reading the article on the history of China in the *Britannica*. It was a long article, about 500,000 words. I'd been chipping away at it for almost a week and I was only up to A.D. 1368, the beginning of the Ming Dynasty. It felt good to have some forced reading time.

I was allowed out of my room for meals, and on Sunday morning I went to church with everyone, but then it was right back to my cell.

At about eight o'clock on Sunday night my

mom came in and sat down on the edge of my bed where I was reading. I knew why she'd come. It was time to get ungrounded. The way I figured, unless you're a teenager with places to go and friends to go with and money to spend when you get there, grounding is a pretty pointless punishment.

And sure enough, Mom's first words were, "Nora, your father and I have decided that your grounding is over. But I don't want you to think we're not concerned about this. This isn't like you, Nora."

I looked up from my book. "Isn't like me? What am I like?"

My mom smiled. "Why, you're sweet and thoughtful, and you want to do your very best at everything, Nora. That's what you're like." I gave a little snort, but Mom ignored the noise. "And if you need help," she continued, "you're smart enough to ask for it."

"I told you, Mom. I don't need any help. And since when have I been *sweet*? Or *thoughtful*?"

Mom stayed focused on her main topic. "But there's nothing wrong with asking for help. We all need help now and then. Besides, you don't want to get a reputation for not caring about your work. Grades are very important, Nora. So, whether you like it or not, first thing tomorrow morning your father and I are going to school to talk with Mrs. Hackney. It's just not right that a perfectly normal student could be allowed to get all Ds. And one C. And your father and I did not get a single academic warning letter from the school, not one. The school has some explaining to do." She paused, her eyes searching my face. "You understand, don't you, Nora? We're not trying to embarrass you. But we have to get to the bottom of this."

I shrugged and said, "Sure. I understand." And I did. I had been certain they would visit the school after they saw those grades.

Mom stood up and started to leave, but she stopped at the door, turned back, and said, "Your dad and I love you, Nora."

I looked up and said, "I love you too."

And that was a fact.

But as I lay there on my bed I wondered if my mom would still be able to say that in a week or two.

six

STAKEOUT

"So are you grounded—like forever?"

That was Stephen's first question when we met at the bus stop Monday morning. He could have tried to telephone on Saturday or Sunday. He didn't call me very often these days, and it was usually just to ask about homework.

"No," I said. "I'm not grounded. Not anymore. But my mom and dad are going to talk to the principal this morning. So stay tuned."

"I don't get it," Stephen said, "how you got such rotten grades. You never do worse than me."

I ignored his bad grammar and shrugged. "Well, I did this time."

I could tell he had more questions, but Lee and Ben came whooping down the street, and Ben shouted, "Hey, Stephen! Guess what—I got forty dollars for my grades, so I got the new Sims game!" And it was like I had disappeared.

That was another thing about fifth grade. Stephen didn't even try to include me when his guy friends were around. But I didn't make it into a big deal. Besides, I had plenty to think about on the bus ride to school.

My first-period class was language arts, and every other Monday Mrs. Noyes took us to the library. Our media center was right across the hall from the main office, so I grabbed a copy of *Time* magazine and got a chair with a clear view of the entrance hall. I pretended to read, but I was on stakeout duty.

At 9:07 my mom and dad showed up. I saw Mrs. Hackney come out of her office and shake hands with each of them. Then they followed her back inside and her door shut behind them.

At 9:14 the intercom in the library chimed, and the school secretary's voice said, "Mrs. Noyes, please come to the main office."

Mrs. Noyes walked across the hall, and the secretary steered her into the principal's office.

At 9:16 Mrs. Noyes hurried out of the office and down the hall toward her classroom. Less than a minute later she was back, still hurrying, and she had something in her hand. It was her green grade book.

I had a pretty good idea what was going on in the principal's office.

At 9:23 my parents left. I ducked behind my magazine in case they looked my way. Then it was all clear.

When Mrs. Noyes came back into the library, I kept my eyes on the page in front of me, but I have good peripheral vision. Mrs. Noyes looked right at me, a long, slow look. And then she went into the librarian's office. She shut the door and started talking to Mrs. Byrne. When I glanced up a minute later they were both looking at me.

By fourth-period math, Mrs. Noyes must have already talked to Mrs. Zhang because after we went over the homework, Mrs. Zhang looked right at me and said, "Nora, are you sure you understand this?" And when she assigned our new work, Mrs. Zhang came over and asked me to do two problems while she watched. She had never done that before.

It was like that all day. All my teachers paid

more attention to me, sort of checking up on me all the time. And I understood exactly why.

Most kids think that if they get bad grades, it's their problem. But that's not true. The fact is, when a kid gets a bad grade, it's like the teacher is getting a bad grade too. And the principal. And the whole school and the whole town and the whole state. And don't forget the parents. A bad grade for a kid is a bad grade for everybody.

After school I hurried to the media center because I wanted to get there before all the computers got reserved.

I'd been staying after school for the extended-day program since first grade, and I could either go to the gym or the library. I almost always went to the library. Stephen did the extended-day program too because both his parents worked, same as mine. But he only went to the library once in a while.

No one was using my favorite computer over in the corner, so I sat down and punched in my password. When the system recognized me, I opened up the Internet browser, went to Google, and typed in "Connecticut Mastery

Testing." There were a ton of Web pages and I found my favorite one. It listed nine ways the state should improve the CMT. I'd been online for about three minutes when Mrs. Byrne came walking toward me, so I switched screens to a kids' page about ocean currents. I didn't want her to know the kind of research I was doing.

Mrs. Byrne smiled and said, "Nora, I just got a call from Mrs. Hackney. She'd like to talk with you in her office."

"Now?" I asked. "Today?"

She nodded. "That's what she said. I'll walk over with you, okay?"

I said, "Sure. Can I leave my things here, or should I bring them?"

"Better bring them," she said, "just to be sure they're safe."

I grabbed my book bag and my jacket. My mind was zooming along at a million miles an hour. This little talk with Mrs. Hackney wasn't in my plan.

But so what? I said to myself. *You knew something like this would happen sooner or later, right? So what if it's a whole lot sooner? No big deal.*

By the time we walked to the principal's office, I had calmed myself down.

No big deal, I told myself again.

Then the door opened.

Wrong. It *was* a big deal. A *very* big deal.

My mom and dad were sitting at the large, round conference table. And Mrs. Noyes. And Mrs. Zhang. And Mrs. Card, the music teacher. And Ms. Prill, the art teacher. And Mr. McKay, the gym teacher. And Dr. Trindler, the guidance counselor.

Mrs. Byrne followed me in and took a seat next to Mrs. Noyes.

And there they sat. All my teachers. And my parents. And the guidance counselor. And the principal.

Mrs. Hackney stood up, and she smiled and nodded at me. I must have had an awful look on my face because she said, "Please, don't be scared, Nora—this is a *very* friendly little group. When your parents stopped in this morning, I decided it would be a good idea for all of us to get together and talk about your report card. Sorry to surprise you, but we didn't want you to worry about it all day—because, honestly, there is absolutely nothing to worry about. Please, take the seat there between your mom and dad. And remember, we're all here because we care about you."

Everyone was smiling and nodding at me as I sat down.

I learned an important fact at that moment: Just because I'm really smart doesn't mean that I can't have a good old-fashioned panic attack.

seven

THE ELEMENT OF SURPRISE

As I sat at the big round table between my mom and dad, I felt like I was trapped in a sandwich. It was mealtime in the principal's office and the main dish was sliced Nora.

Mrs. Hackney liked big meetings. She always had. Almost every other week she called an all-school assembly or an all-fifth-grade meeting or an all-second-grade meeting or some kind of gathering of kids and teachers. She said it gave the school "cohesiveness." She said it created "good group dynamics" for all of us to see each other's faces. And she said meeting as a large group helped us solve our problems all together, all at once. That was clearly what she had in mind today.

Mrs. Hackney sat down and took charge. "Since Mr. and Mrs. Rowley asked for all of you to be here, perhaps they should mention a few of the concerns they shared with me this morning. Then maybe Nora's teachers can explain things from their perspective. And if she wants to, maybe Nora could share a little too. How does that sound?"

My mom nodded and smiled and cleared her throat. She was happy to talk first. Principals and teachers and counselors didn't frighten her one bit. She'd been trying to boss them around for ages—ever since the time she tried to push Ann into the gifted program two years early.

My mom said, "We really appreciate all of you taking the time to come and talk. It's one of the things we've always loved about the Philbrook schools. Our first concern today, apart from Nora's grades themselves, is that we had no warning that there was a problem, not so much as a note or a phone call. And we'd like to understand how that happened."

Nobody said anything for about three seconds.

Then Mrs. Byrne said, "I can only speak about Nora's grade in library skills, of course, but it's pretty clear what happened."

Mrs. Byrne had her grade book open on the table in front of her. So did all my other teachers.

My heart was pounding so hard that I was sure my mom and dad would hear it.

Mrs. Byrne ran her index finger along a row of numbers. "On the first three quizzes and our first reference search, Nora got scores that averaged out to about seventy-two percent, which is a low C. And that's what she had at the seventh week of the term. That's when we mail out academic warnings to parents. And since Nora didn't have a D or lower, there was no warning. Then on the next quiz and our final Internet research project, Nora did quite poorly. And that pulled her grade down. I entered her scores, calculated the average, and there it was." Mrs. Byrne looked at me and smiled. "Nora is one of the library's very best customers, so I didn't like having to give her a D, but that's the way it happened."

Mrs. Zhang nodded. "Exactly," she said. "Numbers are numbers and an average is an average. Same thing in science and math classes for Nora. Her grades dropped off right at the end of the term, and that was it. No warning for you, no warning for me."

All my other teachers started nodding and

agreeing. Mr. McKay cleared his throat and said, "Ditto in gym class. Cs all term, then a big fat F on the obstacle course fitness challenge. Dropped her to a D."

I could tell my dad didn't like it when Mr. McKay said "big fat F." But I sort of enjoyed it. I was proud of that F. I was probably the only kid in the history of the school to fail the obstacle course fitness challenge. It took a lot of creativity to look completely uncoordinated and totally out of shape.

Dr. Trindler said, "I'd like to make an observation." He was the guidance counselor. He was also the psychologist for the school district. He opened a big folder and started shuffling papers around. I knew what that folder was. It was the Nora Rowley folder—all the records from my past five years at Philbrook Elementary School.

As he looked at the papers on the table, Dr. Trindler put the palms of his hands together and then flexed them apart so only the tips of his long, thin fingers were touching—apart, together, apart, together. It made his hands look like a spider doing push-ups on a mirror.

He adjusted his glasses and then tried to smile at my parents. He didn't look at me. "Mr. and Mrs. Rowley, I know this sort of report card can be upsetting, but honestly, grades like this aren't that far out of line with Nora's Mastery Testing profile, or with her academic history here at the elementary school. The Philbrook school system has very high standards. Nora's been an average student, right there in the middle, with room to move either way. And sometimes grades can get tipped downward instead of upward. That's all. And sometimes performance can be related to all sorts of things. Things like unusual stresses at home, like losing a job, or perhaps a death in the family. Sometimes even little disturbances can make a big difference."

Right away my dad leaned forward and said, "Are you pushing this problem back at me? Is that what you're doing? We're not talking about my job or our family life here. You people handed out almost a dozen Ds and you didn't even know what each other was doing. No one stepped up to help a kid who clearly needed some. And now it's somehow *my* fault?

I don't like the sound of that. Not at all."

Mrs. Hackney said, "I'm sure Dr. Trindler didn't mean to make it sound like this was anyone's fault, Mr. Rowley. We're certainly not trying to assign any blame here. We just want to understand what happened so we can make the right adjustments."

My dad didn't sit back, and Mrs. Hackney didn't want to ask him if he had more to say because he probably did. So she kept talking and said, "Well, one person we haven't heard from yet is Nora." Then looking at me, Mrs. Hackney smiled and said, "Nora, is there anything you can tell us that would help us understand what happened at the end of the grading term?"

This meeting wasn't something I had planned for. But it was an interesting opportunity. I had all my teachers and my parents together in one place. I could make a big impression on everyone, all at once. So I tried to stay calm and I decided I needed to say something . . . *remarkable*. I needed to find something surprising, something that would make everybody . . . wonder.

I said, "Umm . . . ," because I was trying to think of something amazing.

And then I said, "Well . . . ," because I was still thinking.

And then I found it—the perfect thing to say.

I said, "Um . . . I guess I didn't do very well in my classes and everything. But I'm not mad about my grades. I like Ds."

I felt my mom and dad stiffen.

Mrs. Hackney paused a moment. Then slowly she said, "You *like* Ds? What do you mean, Nora?"

"You know—Ds," I said. "Ds have a pretty shape." And I kept this blank, happy little smile on my face.

The room went dead silent.

And I realized another fact: When I need to be, I'm a pretty good actor.

Mrs. Hackney was the first person in the audience to come back to life. She said, "That's very . . . interesting, Nora." Mrs. Hackney glanced once around the table. She said, "Well. Perhaps we've all got enough to think about for right now. I know everyone here will be working to help Nora earn better grades in this new term, and I know all our staff will do their best to stay in touch with her parents." She paused and then she said, "There is one other thing, something I talked about with Mr. and Mrs. Rowley this morning. I suggested that it might be helpful if we give Nora some additional evaluation, and they've agreed. That way we can know the best kind of help to offer. So this is a heads-up because Dr. Trindler might need to take Nora out of class now and then over the next few days." Looking around the table with a smile, Mrs. Hackney said, "All right then. If no one has anything else, our little meeting is adjourned. Thank you all for coming."

I looked at the clock. The meeting had only lasted nine minutes. It had felt longer than that. It probably had felt a *lot* longer to my mom and dad.

Out in the hall, my dad said, "Do you have all your things, Nora? I'm going to drop you two off at home." I nodded, so we went out the door.

When we got outside, I had to trot to keep

up with my mom. When we were halfway to the car, she said, "What in the *world* were you talking about in there, Nora? You like the *shape* of Ds?! What did you *mean* by that?"

I shrugged. "Nothing. It was just something to say."

My dad muttered, "More like something that made no sense."

There wasn't much chitchat in the car during the ride home.

So I analyzed the situation, and here's what I came up with:

1. I had a gang of grown-ups thinking about my grades.
2. Plus they were all convinced I was an idiot.
3. My mom was so upset she couldn't chat.
4. My dad was ready to take a punch at someone.
5. The school was going to do some "additional evaluation." Of me.

And I decided that, all in all, it had been a pretty good day.

eight

ROADKILL

There was a dead squirrel in front of the school on Tuesday morning. It had been there awhile, and a group of walkers were out on the sidewalk, cheering whenever it got run over again by a passing car or a bus. It was not a nice way to start the school day, and it didn't exactly make me feel proud to be a human.

In homeroom Mrs. Noyes handed me a note: "Please report to Dr. Trindler's office immediately after lunch and plan to stay there during sixth and seventh periods." Which was lousy news. That was during science and music, two of my favorite classes.

And I knew what would be happening: evaluation. Of me.

We had free reading time at the beginning of first-period language arts, and Stephen came and sat beside me on the pillows in the reading corner. He held up his book and whispered, "I heard about your big meeting yesterday."

"You did?" I asked. "How?"

"How?" said Stephen. "'Cause it's all over the school, that's how. I heard that Jenny Ashton was in the nurse's room after school. She saw Mrs. Byrne take you to the office, and she saw all the teachers. And your mom and dad. Everyone knows you got bad grades, too. I guess that's kind of my fault. 'Cause I told Ellen and she told Jenny. Sorry about that. And I'm *really* sorry you're in so much trouble. Did they yell at you and stuff?"

"Of course they didn't," I said. "And I'm not in trouble."

Stephen frowned and said, "You sure? 'Cause my mom would put me in a military school or something if I even got *one* D, let alone a bunch of 'em. And Jenny said you were crying when you came out of the office, and your mom was dragging you by the arm."

"*What*?! That's a lie!" and I said it so loud that Mrs. Noyes looked up from her book and frowned at me. So I pretended to read until the coast was clear, and then I hissed, "No one yelled at all, and no one even came close to crying, least of all me. *Oooh!*—that Jenny Ashton is gonna *get* it!"

Stephen needed more proof that I hadn't

been tortured in the meeting. He said, "So . . . if they didn't yell at you, what did everyone say?"

"Nothing much," I whispered. "My mom wanted to know how come she didn't get any warnings about my Ds. And the teachers had to explain why I got the bad grades. It was all pretty stupid. I got bad grades because I did bad on some tests—duh. And now they want me to take more tests to see if I'm as dumb as they think I am."

"But you're not dumb," Stephen said. "Even *I* know that, and I really *am* dumb."

I pushed him on the arm. "Don't *ever* say that, Stephen. I *hate* it when you say that."

He shrugged. "You're the one who always says you have to face facts. So face it: I'm dumb."

I pushed him again, and that was one too many disturbances.

"Nora." Mrs. Noyes was using her soft, reading-time voice. "Either read quietly or I will find you some other work and another place to sit. Final warning."

I nodded and put my nose in my book. But I

whispered to Stephen, "Bad test grades do *not* mean you are dumb, and I am *not* in trouble—and if you see that Jenny Ashton, you tell her to start fixing those rotten rumors before I fix her!"

When I went to my locker after first period, Charlotte Kendall came up to me. Charlotte wears a different colored ribbon in her hair every day, and she always holds her books and her notebook up tight against her stomach with both arms. She whispered, but Charlotte's whisper carries about ten feet. So we had an audience.

"Nora—I *heard* about your grades. Your averages—they must be *ruined*! What are you going to do? Do you think you're going to get left back? I couldn't *stand* it if you got left back."

I smiled as best as I could. "It's okay, Charlotte. I won't get left back, I promise."

"Well," she said, "if there's *anything* I can help you with, just ask me, okay? Because I got almost straight As, and I really would help you if you wanted, okay?"

I looked hard at Charlotte, testing for acid

in her face or her eyes. Not a trace—only sweetness. Charlotte meant every word. And she wasn't bragging about her grades, just stating a fact.

So I smiled and said, "Thanks, Charlotte. That means a lot to me." And it did. Charlotte truly felt bad for me. She helped me remember that as far as everyone else was concerned, I was going through a crisis, an ordeal.

Because for everyone else it was an absolute fact that fifth-grade grades mattered. My grades made me look like that dead *Sciurus carolinensis* on the road out in front of the school.

And in less than three hours, Dr. Trindler was going to get out his measuring tools and try to figure out just how flat this squirrel really was.

nine

CORNERED

It was raining at lunchtime, so I got a pass to go to the library. Indoor recess in the gym was always noisy and confused, and the library was always just the opposite.

I went to a table near the back wall to do my math homework. I was whipping through the sixth problem when a voice said, "Nora?"

I jumped a mile. I hadn't heard Mrs. Byrne come up behind me. She smiled and said, "Sorry to startle you. Sometimes this carpet is almost too quiet. May I talk with you over at the front desk?"

"Sure," I said, and I got up and followed her.

She said, "Back here," and she motioned me behind the desk to the long work counter. "I want you to read something I printed out yesterday." Then she handed me ten or fifteen pieces of paper that were stapled together.

I knew instantly. I knew what I was holding. I pretended to read the first sheet, but I hardly saw the words. My thinking had kicked up into overdrive. I was in trouble. I needed a way out. I needed a major distraction—something like a fire drill, or maybe an earthquake.

It took a lot of effort not to start breathing fast, and I was afraid my cheeks would turn bright red. I turned to the second page and then the third, barely reading, just stalling for time.

Finally I had to say something, so I said, "It looks like a list."

Mrs. Byrne said, "Turn to page five, Nora, and read some of the entries out loud—but please keep your voice down."

I skipped ahead and started to read. "'MIT Internet Registration home page; Issues in light wave theory; JaneGoodall.org home page; Fuel cell technology comes of age; Hybrid vehicles find new homes; Cold fusion anomalies; Field Museum Egyptology Department; Richard Feynman's lecture on—'"

Mrs. Byrne interrupted and said, "Thank you, Nora. That's enough. Can you tell me what you've been reading?"

"Something from the computer, right?" I looked into her face.

She wasn't buying my innocent act. N
even a little bit.

Mrs. Byrne shook her head. "It's more like something from *your* computer, Nora. More precisely, that information is stored under your login account on the media center's main server. When I began to back up the system yesterday afternoon, one terminal was still active—the one in the corner. I went to shut it down, but something on the Internet browser caught my eye, something about the Connecticut Mastery Tests. I didn't remember any teachers using that terminal, so I checked the login name, and it was you, Nora. You forgot to log out when you went to the meeting in Mrs. Hackney's office. I know you might think I was prying, but it's part of my job to monitor the Internet activity of all student accounts. So I looked around a little."

Mrs. Byrne looked me right in the eye. She said, "What you're holding there are the first thirteen pages of a 159-page document that lists the Web pages you have visited or accessed since the beginning of this school year. Your files are using *five gigabytes* of storage space on the rver. Do you know what that means, Nora? I think you do, but I'll tell you anyway. It means that so far this school year you have gathered more information for access and retrieval than all the rest of the fourth- and fifth-grade students combined. Just glancing through the Web pages of the links you have in your hands there, it appears that you have done extensive research on alternative energy sources; you have been trading e-mails with a primate expert at the Jane Goodall Institute; you have a keen interest in educational theory; and apparently you have been enrolled in a college-level astronomy course over the Internet at Massachusetts Institute of Technology."

Again she paused. Then, speaking slowly, Mrs. Byrne said, "But the most interesting thing to me is the fact that *you* are the child who failed her basic Internet research project three weeks ago—and therefore got a D in library skills. So, Nora. How should I be thinking about all this new information?"

Mrs. Byrne had me. I was trapped.

When an animal gets backed into a corner, zoologists say the animal will usually choose one of three instinctive responses. But I've never considered myself an animal. I wasn't going to fight, or run away, or play dead. This was not the time for instincts. I had to think my way out of this corner.

It's not a coincidence that cartoons show an idea as a lightbulb. Because when an idea hits, it feels like someone has flipped a big switch.

And an idea blasted me, right there in front of Mrs. Byrne—instant light. Yes, I was certainly in a corner. But it wasn't a small corner, and I didn't really have to get out of it. There was plenty of room in the corner for someone to join me.

In fact, I decided that it actually might be good to have someone else in my corner.

ten

FOR NOW

I had seen Mrs. Byrne almost every school day since the beginning of first grade—more than seven hundred school days. A lot of those days I had spent more time in the same room with Mrs. Byrne than I had with my mom or dad. So I'd had plenty of time to form a clear opinion about her. And in my opinion, Mrs. Byrne was one of the best people in the whole school. I had never seen her lose her temper, and she always seemed fair and open-minded. Which makes sense—why would a narrow-minded person be a librarian?

And now Mrs. Byrne was standing in front of me, waiting. She wanted me to explain why a kid who just got a bunch of Ds was exploring so many challenging subjects on the Internet.

One of the first things I learned at school was how to read a teacher's face. It's a school survival skill and all kids become experts at it. But as we stood there face-to-face in the library—me looking up, her looking down—I could not figure out what was going on behind Mrs. Byrne's greenish brown eyes.

So I started off cautiously. I said, "I like to read about a lot of things."

She smiled slightly. "I already know that much, Nora. I want to know about your grades. It's perfectly clear to me now that you are not a below-average student, or even an average student. Far from it. And you've been hiding that from me and everyone else at school." She paused with her head tilted as she figured out something else. Then she said, "And your parents don't know how bright you are either, do they?" I shook my head. "So why have you been keeping this a secret?" she asked.

I told her the truth in the simplest way I could. I said, "I didn't want to be different all the time. I mean, I *am* different, and I know that. I just didn't want everyone else to treat me that way. Because it's not their business."

Mrs. Byrne nodded slowly. "I can understand that, I think. But why the low grades?"

I had to trust her. I had no choice. I said, "I

did that on purpose. I'm trying to do something . . . about grades. Everyone makes way too big a deal about them."

Mrs. Byrne's eyebrows scrunched together above her nose. She shook her head and said, "But why get Ds? How can that help?"

"Well," I said, "those Ds already have my teachers and my parents and the principal thinking and talking about grades, right? And I hope they're going to think a lot more about grades. And tests, too. Because I've got sort of a . . . a plan." Then I looked her right in the eye and said, "Except if you tell on me, I don't think it will work."

No expression. "What are you trying to accomplish with this . . . plan?"

"Nothing bad," I said quickly. I almost started to tell about Stephen, but I didn't. I didn't want anyone to think he was involved. So I said, "Most kids never talk about it, but a lot of the time bad grades make them feel dumb, and almost all the time it's not true. And good grades can make other kids think that they're better, and that's not true either. And then all the kids start competing and comparing. The smart kids feel smarter and better and get all stuck-up, and the regular kids feel stupid and like there's no way to ever catch up. And the people who are supposed to help kids, the parents and the teachers, they don't. They just add more pressure and keep making up more and more tests."

Mrs. Byrne's eyes flashed and she shook her head sharply. "But the teachers don't like all this testing either. And I was *not* happy when they made me start giving grades in library skills. That's not what the library is for. So don't think it's only the teachers. It's the school boards. And the state. And the federal government, too."

Then her pale cheeks colored, just a hint. Mrs. Byrne tried to hide it, but she was embarrassed by that outburst. She hadn't meant to show me what she was feeling.

But she had.

I pretended not to notice. I said, "Well, anyway, we have to have the tests and the grades, and of course the grades are going to be used to sort us into different levels in sixth grade—the smart kids and the dumb kids. And I don't like the way it's done and I want to try to change some things."

Mrs. Byrne said, "Isn't this dangerous? For you, I mean. Getting such bad grades?"

I said, "Maybe. But it's sort of like I have immunity. I'm smart, and I know I'm smart, and I know that when I have to prove I'm smart, I'll be able to. My grades won't matter so much, not like they do now for a lot of kids. And even if I do get into some trouble, I don't care. I'm not doing this for fun. And I'm not doing it for myself." I paused, and then I said, "And I think I can do it without any help . . . at least, I hope so."

That was bait. And Mrs. Byrne knew I was fishing. And she went for the hook anyway.

"What sort of help do you think you might need?"

And I knew. I had been right about Mrs. Byrne. She was one of the good guys.

I smiled up into her face. "You'd do that? You'd help me?"

Mrs. Byrne said, "I didn't say that. But I can't see any school rules that you've broken. Your parents would probably like to know they've got a brilliant child living in their house, and I certainly think you should tell them. But that's between you and them." Her eyes searched my face. "I don't know if I could help you in any direct way. But there's nothing in my job description that requires me to report on every conversation I have with every student. So this can be between us. At least for now. Do you understand?"

I nodded. "Yes, and that's a big help . . . for now. Thanks, Mrs. Byrne."

She nodded and smiled at me, but just barely. Underneath that smile she was worried. I wasn't sure if she was worried for me or for herself.

Probably for both of us.

eleven

MOUNTED UNDER GLASS

"Nora! Welcome!"

It was the beginning of fifth period. Dr. Trindler motioned me to a chair across from him at a square table. He seemed a little too happy, but I didn't mind. I was his big project for the afternoon, and I figured that the man must love his work.

Dr. Trindler had two jobs. He was the guidance counselor for our school, but he was also the psychologist for the three elementary schools and the junior high school in Philbrook. Plaques and diplomas and certificates covered two walls of the office, all of them mounted under glass like some flat, colorless butterfly collection.

As my eyes jumped from rectangle to rectangle, suddenly I pictured myself pressed thin as paper, trapped in a frame on his wall, my nose jammed against a sheet of glass. And then I saw myself like a specimen between two glass slides, with Dr. Trindler peering at me throu a microscope. I pushed those thoughts away.

Dr. Trindler's assistant was Mrs. Drummond. She was the counselor when he was out working at other schools. She sat at a desk about ten feet away from the table where I was sitting, but she was in a different room on the other side of a wall that was mostly one big window.

"So," Dr. Trindler said, "are you ready for some fun today?"

I nodded. "Sure, I guess so." But I still felt like a sheet of glass was pushing on my nose.

"Good," he said. "Then let's get going. I'd like to give you a test, but it's not like a regular classroom test. It's a test that'll help me and all your teachers understand the best way for you to learn, okay?"

I nodded and he kept talking. "We'll start with some questions. I'll read them out loud one at a time, and you'll answer each one as best as you can. And I'll keep track of your answers on this sheet, okay?"

I nodded again and said, "Okay." I could see the sheet he was writing on. On the upper

…ıt-hand corner it said WISC III. I knew what …ıat meant. Dr. Trindler was giving me an IQ test. On an IQ test you get a score, and then sometimes they divide your score by your age. Which is why IQ means Intelligence Quotient, because of the division. It's kind of complicated, and I had only read a little about IQ testing on the Internet.

And that's why I started to get worried about this test. The Connecticut Mastery Testing had been easy. I got an average score because I had been able to look up the scoring information on the Internet. That's the way I knew how many to get right and how many to miss on each part.

This test was different. I had never seen it before.

Dr. Trindler didn't waste any time. First he asked me a bunch of questions, and I had to answer them out loud. And I had to group some things into categories, then do some math problems, then match a bunch of word definitions, then answer more questions about what I'd do in different situations, and then I had to remember the order of some numbers

and repeat them back to him. Then I looked
pictures and had to say what was missing, and
I had to copy marks from one page to another,
and then mess around with some colored
blocks and some puzzles. The test went on and
on—over a dozen different parts. It took
almost two hours to finish.

And all the time I was worried. I didn't
know how I was doing on this test—because I
didn't want my score to be too high. Or too
low, either.

All I could think of was to try to mess up on
three questions out of every ten. That made
sense to me. I figured that would keep my
score at about seventy percent, and that would
be like a C—which would be normal. I kept
watching Dr. Trindler's face for clues to see
how I was doing, but it was like he had a mask
on.

And then finally he said, "There. We're all
done—that wasn't so bad, was it?"

I shook my head and said, "No. It was fine."
Then I said, "When will I get to see my
scores?"

"That will be up to your parents, Nora. On

...s kind of test we never give the scores to the ...tudent."

I couldn't believe it. I said, "You mean I have to take the test, but I don't get to see the score?"

He shrugged and smiled. "It's just the way it is with a test like this. Your score is sort of like a tool, something for me and Mrs. Hackney and your parents to use. You really don't have to worry about it at all."

I felt myself getting angry, because I hate stuff like that—when grown-ups treat kids like they're stupid. Or like they can't be trusted. It's very annoying. Smart old Dr. Trindler with the long, skinny fingers could know my scores because he had all that paper hanging on his wall. But me, the kid who just beat her brains out for two hours, *I* wasn't allowed to know anything.

And I said to myself, *But so what? Grownups run everything and it stinks and there's nothing kids can do about it because that's the way it's always been and that's the way it's always going to be. Big news.*

Then I caught myself.

I hate to catch myself thinking like that. That kind of attitude has a name. It's called being cynical. It comes from the Greek word for dog, *kunikos*. Because there was this bunch of losers in ancient Greece, sort of a club, called the Cynics. The Cynics had no respect for anything or anybody. Like a dog who chews up your best shoes and then wags his tail. Or makes a mess on your front lawn right while you're watching. The *kunikos* doesn't care and it does what it wants to, and it assumes everyone else is the same way it is.

But I had caught myself. I didn't let myself be cynical. Because that's too easy. And because I knew better.

People like Dr. Trindler didn't do things because they're mean. Or cynical. They did things because most of the time they actually believed those were the right things to do. He thought it was bad for someone like me to know my own IQ score. And maybe he was right. If the score was low, then I might think I was stupid. And if the score was high, then I might think I was better than somebody else.

But then I asked myself, *How are these IQ*

scores different from grades? Or the Mastery Testing scores? How come they don't hide all the grades and scores from kids? Teachers need to know the grades so they can figure out how to help kids do better and learn more, but why do kids need to know them? After all, those CMT scores didn't help Stephen—not one bit.

Anyway, Dr. Trindler said good-bye and Mrs. Drummond wrote me a pass to go to last period. And after two hours of thinking, gym class was wonderful because all during the fall we played soccer almost every day.

When I was three years old I saw a soccer game for the first time on the local Spanish TV channel, and I went nuts for it. I loved the way the camera showed almost the whole field at once. I could see the players plan and make plays. And I could see the math, too—the crossing lines as a striker sped up to meet a flying corner kick, and the angles as midfielders passed the ball so it was always just beyond a defender's toe. I saw angles again as players blocked passes and cut off shooters. Each shot on goal was a balance of velocity and trajectory. It was all math and physics in motion.

And soccer was such a mental game. The best players had the whole field and all the other players completely inside their heads. The field wasn't out there. It was all inside. And then, *"Goooooooooooool!"* Fantastic!

Ever since first grade the soccer field had been the only place where I really let myself loose. I had never had to hide anything out on the soccer field. I could be as smart and creative and talented as I wanted to—because nobody ever treats a gifted athlete like she's weird. And that's not true if you're a gifted student.

So during gym class it was me, four other girls, and six boys against another mixed team of eleven kids. And Stephen was on my team. It was a good, quick game, and we won it four goals to three. I scored two of our four goals.

But the best part wasn't the winning or the praise from Mr. McKay or the high fives from my teammates. I hadn't been trying to beat anyone or prove I was great.

For me the best part came when the game was tied at three all, and there were less than two minutes on the clock. With my hair pulled back into a ponytail and my legs and arms and lungs pumping away, I felt like I was a hundred feet above the field, calmly looking down. The need to think and analyze and plot and plan melted away. Ideas were the same as actions, and I didn't have to hold anything back. And when Stephen sent me a perfect pass, I drove to the center, dribbled through three defenders, and then beat the goalie.

It was pure play—no questions, no worries, no walls, no frames hanging on nails, no sheets of glass trying to press me down flat.

For twenty-five minutes on that Tuesday afternoon, I was free.

twelve

INTELLIGENCE

On Wednesday morning at the end of home-room, Mrs. Noyes called me up to her desk.

"Nora, Mrs. Byrne wants you to bring all your overdue books back to the library before noon."

I said, "But nothing's overdue."

Mrs. Noyes said, "Well, you'll have to tell that to Mrs. Byrne."

And then I understood the message.

Mrs. Byrne didn't need to see me about overdue books. There was some other reason. And for the first time, it struck me how good it was to have someone else know the real me. And also how strange and new it felt to have someone else know that I wasn't . . . normal. Then I thought of a good tongue twister: No more normal Nora—five times fast.

All that ran through my mind in less than a second, so I nodded to Mrs. Noyes and said, "Okay. I'll go to the library right now," and I started to leave.

Then Mrs. Noyes said, "Oh—another thing, Nora. I saw Dr. Trindler in the teacher's room this morning. He wants you to come to his office again this afternoon during fifth period." I was halfway out the door by then, so I just nodded and said, "Fifth period. Okay."

When I got to the library, Mrs. Byrne was busy checking out books for a third-grade class. But she caught my eye and motioned me over to the front desk.

"Here, Nora," and she handed me a stack of student name cards. "Would you sort these alphabetically, please?"

I said, "Sure." There was another chair, but it was easier to sort the cards standing up.

About three minutes later all the third graders were gone, but Mrs. Byrne was still busy. Without taking her eyes off the computer screen, she said, "That test—the one you took yesterday with Dr. Trindler? What was that like?"

"Kind of fun," I said. "It was an IQ test. First time I've had a test like that."

Mrs. Byrne kept tapping on her keyboard. "And how do you think you did?" she asked.

I said, "Well, I tried to get about three things wrong out of every ten. It was all I could figure out to do. I was trying to get about seventy percent right. You know, about average."

Mrs. Byrne said, "I see."

She started sorting through some papers, but her hands were all jerky and nervous. Then she stopped and looked me right in the eye. "I found something out this morning. The test you took was scaled for children up to sixteen and a half years old. Your score translated to an IQ of one hundred and seventeen, and that's above average."

I interrupted and said, "That's not really a big problem, is it? I mean, tests like this aren't always right, are they?"

Mrs. Byrne said, "There's more to it than that. One hundred and seventeen? That's what your IQ would be if you were sixteen years old. But since you're only eleven, your score translates to a higher IQ. Much higher. According to that test, you have an IQ of *one hundred and eighty-eight*. That's way up near the top of the scale. And Dr. Trindler doesn't know what to think."

My legs felt a little weak. I sat down. "What . . . what else did Dr. Trindler say to you?"

Mrs. Byrne shook her head. "He didn't tell me anything at all. He hasn't talked about this to anyone but his assistant, Mrs. Drummond. The only reason I know is because Mrs. Drummond's car is in the shop. We live near each other, so I drove her to school today. And she was bursting to tell someone. Dr. Trindler said your IQ contradicts your whole academic record, so he thinks the test must be wrong."

Mrs. Byrne stopped talking and pressed her lips together into a frown. She said, "I know I shouldn't be telling you this, Nora. But I couldn't help it."

"I won't tell anyone you told me."

She smiled. "I know that, Nora. That's not what I'm worried about. You're getting yourself into a tricky situation here. I don't want you to get . . . hurt. I don't want anyone to get hurt."

We were both quiet. Then Mrs. Byrne said, "So what do you think you'll do?"

I shrugged and tried to smile a little. "I have to see what Dr. Trindler says. I have to go there again for fifth period."

Mrs. Byrne said, "He could be planning another test for today."

I stood up and said, "Well, I won't know until I get there. And right now I guess I'd better get to art class. May I have a pass?"

"Of course you may," she said. Then she gave me a big smile, a real one, and she said, "I don't think I would have ever been brave enough to try something like this when I was a girl, Nora. Even now, I think I'm more worried than you are!"

I smiled back. "Don't be worried. Tests and grades don't matter that much—remember?"

Mrs. Byrne laughed and said, "That's right. I'm sure there's nothing to worry about."

She handed me the pass and I said, "Thanks, Mrs. Byrne."

And I didn't mean just for the pass. And she knew that.

And she said, "You're so welcome, Nora."

thirteen

AN OBSERVATION

It was Wednesday, so the smell of almost-spaghetti filled the cafeteria. I sat with my friend Karen and five or six other girls. We ate at our regular table, right next to the one where Stephen and his friends usually sat.

I'm not proud of this, but I've always been an eavesdropper. I've never gone out of my way to eavesdrop—except maybe once or twice. But if I happen to be close enough, and if people happen to be talking loud enough, I always listen. If people want to keep secrets, they should learn how to whisper.

I probably wouldn't have started listening to the boys sitting behind me, but I heard Merton Lake say, "Don't be such an idiot—no one will ever travel to the sun. It's a huge bunch of burning gas, stupid." We had been learning about the solar system in science class, and I had been doing some research about the sun on my own. So when Merton said that, my ears perked up.

Then Stephen said, "Still, I bet someone could go there one day. Like maybe if the sun gets cooler."

"Yeah," said Merton. "Or 'like maybe' if they can find someone as dumb as you to volunteer!"

And then all the other guys at the table started laughing.

I wanted to turn around and tackle that Merton Lake, knock him right onto the floor. He was one of the smartest boys in fifth grade and also my least favorite. Merton had been in our fourth-grade class, too, and he had gotten one of the highest scores on the Mastery Tests. After he found out Stephen's score, he teased him about it for a month, calling him names like "retard" and "brain-dead."

This year Merton was in the gifted program, and he loved coming back from his special classes so he could show off about what he had learned. Plus, he had already announced to anybody who would listen that his big brother and his dad and his grandfather had all gone to Harvard University, and that he was going to go there too. One kid like Merton can almost ruin a whole school year.

But one of the great things about Stephen is that he keeps on trying. Even before the other boys had stopped laughing at him, he said, "But how about when all the gas is used up? The sun'll have to go out someday and then I bet someone could go there."

I didn't have to turn around to see the nasty smirk on Merton's face. I could hear it in his voice. "Nice try, *moron*. The sun's never going to burn out."

And the rest of the boys kept on laughing.

It was too much, hearing him treat Stephen that way. A new fact burst into my mind: The only way to stop a kid like Merton is to over-power him. And something inside me snapped.

I whipped around on my lunch stool and I jabbed my pointer finger toward Merton's face and I said, "You are *wrong*, Merton! Wrong! The sun *will* go out. The sun is using up its sup-ply of hydrogen because the hydrogen atoms are being converted into helium atoms. And that atomic conversion is *not* the same as burn-ing gas, which is what you just said, *moron*. And only seven tenths of one percent of the available hydrogen actually converts into heat energy, and the best estimate is that it will take another one hundred billion years for all the hydrogen to be used up. So at the end of one hundred billion years, the sun will, in fact, *go out*. So Stephen is right. And more important than that, *you* are *WRONG*! So just stop acting like you are the most brilliant person in the solar system and do everyone a big favor and shut up and eat the rest of that disgusting spaghetti!"

When my speech ended, I was the center of a circle of silence. All around me forkloads of food hung halfway between plates and open mouths. Straws were stuck between lips, but no one was drinking. Nothing moved except little cubes of red Jell-O wiggling in plastic bowls.

And all eyes were on me. And maybe on Merton, too. But mostly on me.

Karen broke the spell. "Give it up for Nora!" And she started chanting, "Nora, Nora, Nora," and the other girls at my table started chanting too, and it went on for about ten seconds until Mrs. Rosen walked over and made everyone quiet down.

I felt terrible. I had never lost my temper in public before, and I had never used my intelligence that way either. Merton had deserved every word I had thrown into his face, but I had gone too far.

And what would Stephen think? I had *never* seen him get mad, not once.

I had to get out of there. I stood up and grabbed my tray. But as I turned around, something caught my eye.

Someone was standing by the door to the playground, about ten feet from where I had been sitting—close enough to have heard every word I'd said.

It was Dr. Trindler.

fourteen

CHANGES

At the beginning of fifth period Dr. Trindler was waiting for me. No smiles this time, no pleasant chatter. He was sitting behind his desk, all business. He pointed at the chair across from him and said, "Please sit down."

Mrs. Drummond was at her desk on the other side of the big window. She was trying to look busy, but I could tell she was tuned in like we were the final episode of her favorite TV show.

Dr. Trindler sat there for almost half a minute, doing that spidery thing with his fingers. Then he said, "Can we talk honestly to each other, Nora?"

"Sure," I said.

He leaned forward with his elbows on the desk. "I had been planning to give you another test today. But fifteen minutes ago I observed you speaking to Merton Lake in the cafeteria. And now I don't think another test is really necessary. Do you?"

I shrugged. "I don't know."

He raised his eyebrows and one long index finger and said, "Remember? We are talking *honestly* with each other, Nora. I want to know if you think I need to give you another test today."

I said, "Depends on what you want to find out."

He smiled and said, "That's easy: I want to find out if the score you got on yesterday's test is accurate. What do you think—was that an accurate score?"

I shook my head. "Probably not."

Dr. Trindler leaned farther forward. "And why is that?"

I didn't answer. Everything was moving too fast. I needed time to think.

Dr. Trindler thought he already knew I was a genius. And he also thought that I knew that he knew. But he really didn't know anything, not for sure. So I thought, *Maybe I can bluff my way out of this. Maybe I can take another test and really mess it up. Then Dr. Trindler couldn't prove anything—except that he's a lousy test-giver. Or maybe I could . . .*

And then I stopped. I just stopped.

I was tired of it. I was tired of always holding back. I was tired of acting like I didn't understand things. I was tired of pretending to be average. It wasn't true.

Dr. Trindler repeated his question. "Why do you think yesterday's test score wasn't accurate, Nora?"

I looked him right in the eye. "Because the score is too low. Everything I missed, I missed on purpose."

Dr. Trindler's mind tried to process that, and I could see him trying to recalculate my IQ in his head. And he couldn't do it.

So I said, "The simplest way to estimate a more accurate score is to increase the raw score to the ninety-ninth percentile range and then adjust for my age. Because I don't think I would have missed more than one or two questions on the whole test—not if I had wanted to do my best."

Dr. Trindler thought about that for a second and said, "But why didn't you want to do your best?"

I didn't say anything, so he said, "And I don't

understand about your report card, either. Can you tell me a little about that—about all the Ds?"

I didn't want to have this talk with Dr. Trindler. I knew what he wanted. He wanted to have a deep conversation with me. He wanted to work up a theory about me. And about my problem. Maybe try to link my behavior to some incident in my past. Or maybe it was my mom and dad's fault. Or maybe I had deep hidden fears.

And I knew enough about psychology to know that Dr. Trindler would never get it right. Because my reasons would be too simple. Not wanting to be pushed to "achieve" all the time was *not* some psychological problem I was having. It was an intelligent choice. And if I had been "working up to my potential," could I have ever been best friends with a regular kid like Stephen? Fat chance.

I changed the subject. "Are you going to give me another test?"

He said, "No. I don't think so." Dr. Trindler paused and then he said, "You know that I'm going to share my findings with Mrs. Hackney, don't you?"

I nodded.

He said, "And you understand why I need to tell her about your scores?"

I said, "Sure. My mom and dad asked for the testing, and the school has to give them my scores, and it's Mrs. Hackney's job to tell them."

Dr. Trindler nodded. "That's correct."

He paused again, waiting for me to keep talking. But I didn't.

So he said, "Is there anything you'd like to talk about, Nora?"

I shook my head. "No thanks."

"Well," he said, "if something does come up, and if you think I might be a help, you can always find me, okay?"

I nodded and said, "Okay." And I smiled a little because I could tell Dr. Trindler just wanted to help.

A minute later I was walking through the empty hallways, headed for Mrs. Zhang's room and the second half of science class. It was still the same day, and it was the same school with the same teachers and the same kids.

But something was different.

Me.

fifteen

PARTNERSHIP

Mrs. Hackney had called my mom at work right after school, so by dinnertime on Wednesday my whole family knew everything that Dr. Trindler had discovered.

Our evening meal was a smorgasbord of emotions.

Mom and Dad didn't know whether to be mad at me for keeping a secret from them, or to be thrilled that I was a genius and not some idiot who thought Ds had a pretty shape. My mom said, "Isn't this *exciting?* If we can get an admissions interview, and if Nora does well on the entrance tests, I bet she could get into Chelborn Academy—maybe even get a scholarship. And from there, who knows? Our little Nora could end up at Princeton—or even Yale or Harvard!"

I could tell Ann didn't like that idea one bit. She had been the star student all her life. But she pretended she wasn't interested and she said, "I knew that Nora was smart all along."

And when Todd heard the news, he rolled his eyes and said, "Just what I need around here—another smart sister."

I let everyone else do the talking during dinner. And I didn't volunteer any more information about my report card. When my mom said, "I guess I understand a little better about those bad grades now," I just smiled and nodded.

Because that wasn't part of the deal. Yes, now they knew I wasn't an average kid, and they figured out that for years I had been getting average grades on purpose. But my reasons for getting those Ds—they didn't need to know about that.

I faced the fact that my plan was ruined. Everyone would be watching me now. All my teachers would know I was smart. And it probably wouldn't be long before the whole fifth grade would know about me too. School is no place to try to keep a secret.

After dinner I went to my room to read, and about eight o'clock Todd yelled upstairs, "Hey Nora—it's your *boyfriend* on the phone."

I picked up the portable phone in the hall and took it into my room.

"Hello?"

"Hi, Nora." Stephen didn't have to say his name because he was the only boy who ever called me.

From downstairs Todd made a big, wet, kissing sound into the phone, and in a high voice that was supposed to sound like me, he said, "Oh *Stephen*, I'm *so* glad you called—I've been missing you *all* night."

"Todd!" I said. "You are such a jerk!" Then I yelled, "Mom! Make Todd hang up the phone!" The kitchen phone clattered onto its cradle and I said, "Sorry. Todd's not winning any prizes for maturity this week."

Stephen said, "Maturity? Well, how about you? That thing you did in the lunchroom today wasn't exactly cool either." He sounded mad.

I hadn't been ready for an attack and that's what it felt like. I said, "But . . . but I couldn't stand it. You heard Merton—he was being awful. And . . . and I had to make him stop."

Stephen said, "But he wasn't talking to you,

Nora. He wasn't even sitting at your table. It was none of your business. I don't need anybody to take care of me."

I said, "But if someone was attacking me and making everybody laugh at me, wouldn't you help me? If you could? Wouldn't you?"

That stopped him. He said, "I . . . I guess so." Then he thought a little and said, "But it wasn't like that, Nora. We were just talking. And I'm not afraid of being laughed at. And besides, everybody knows that Merton's a stupid creep. Nobody takes him seriously. All you did was make yourself look like a fool."

It hurt when Stephen said that. I didn't say anything.

"Nora?"

I didn't answer.

Stephen blew a big breath out through his mouth. Then he said, "Listen, I'm sorry I called you a fool, okay? I'm sorry . . . okay? And what you said to Merton? It was really pretty great." Then Stephen paused a few seconds and said, "Actually, I wish *I* could have said all that."

I waited another second or two. "Honest?" I asked.

He said, "Honest. And how did you know all that extra stuff about the sun and everything?"

A new fact was staring me in the face: I knew I would never have a better chance than this moment to tell Stephen the truth—the facts of me. And I also knew that if Stephen didn't hear the truth directly from me, it would be bad.

So I said, "That stuff about the sun? I . . . I did some extra reading. It's sort of complicated. But listen . . . I've got to explain something—something important."

I told Stephen everything. About how I had learned to read when I was two and a half, and the way I had only pretended to learn how to read when we were in first grade. I told him how I had kept all my test scores lower, and how even my own family hadn't known how smart I was. I explained the way I had missed questions on the Mastery Testing on purpose. I told him how Mrs. Byrne had found my computer files and then kept my secret. And I even told him about Dr. Trindler and the IQ test.

When I was done, Stephen was quiet. Then he said, "So how smart are you?"

"Well," I said, "Dr. Trindler thinks I'm a genius."

"Are you? Are you a *genius*?"

I could hear it in Stephen's voice. What I'd always been afraid of. Stephen was already starting to think I was weird. Weird Nora, the genius girl.

And I knew that the next couple of sentences would be important.

I said, "I guess I am. But so what? So what if I'm a genius? I'm still me, Stephen. It's not like I'm any different."

"Yeah? Well, what about at lunch today?" he asked. "That was pretty different."

"Okay. Yeah, that was kind of different. But if I hadn't just told you everything else, would you have started to think I had turned into this totally different person or something? I'm still *me*. No matter what, I'm still me."

There was only the hum of the open phone line. Then Stephen said, "But . . . but it's like you've been a *spy* . . . for years. Like you've been this genius secret agent, spying on all the regular kids. And all those Ds on your report card? I was really worried about you, and all the time you were just goofing around!"

"No!" I said. "That's the thing, Stephen—I *wasn't* goofing around. I got those Ds on purpose. Because I got mad about the way everyone makes such a big deal about grades. And test scores, too. I had a plan. And now it's completely ruined and I'm in all kinds of trouble. So how much of a genius could I really be?"

Stephen said, "You had a plan? What kind of a plan?"

"It's all messed up now," I said. "But . . . I just wanted to show everybody that bad grades don't mean a kid isn't smart, and that good grades don't always mean a kid is so smart either. And I thought the teachers liked giving all the tests and grades and everything. But Mrs. Byrne told me that that's not really true. A lot of the teachers don't like all the competition and the testing, especially the Mastery Tests. Like I said, my plan was lousy from the start."

Again the only sound was the hiss of the telephone. Then Stephen began talking—slowly at first and then faster. He said, "Everybody's going to find out now, right? They're going to know that you're really smart, aren't they?"

"Yeah," I said, "I guess so."

"Like all our teachers will know, and Mrs. Hackney? And the kids, too—*everybody*, right?"

I said, "Yeah. Everybody."

"Listen! Everybody's going to know you're this genius now, so everyone thinks you're going to *be* that way—supersmart, right? And they're all gonna think that now you'll get great grades and do the gifted program and stuff, right?"

"Yeah," I said. "Probably. Especially my parents."

Stephen could barely get the words out, he was talking so fast. He said, "So that's what everybody's gonna expect now, right? This super-supersmart kid. But what if you don't *do* that? What if you don't do what everybody expects—like . . . like you break the regular rules about being smart? And you start playing by *different* rules—*your* rules!" He paused, waiting for my reaction. But he couldn't wait. "See what I mean?" he asked. "Do you get it?"

Stephen's idea wasn't like a lightbulb turning on—it was like a blast from a laser cannon. I almost shouted, "Stephen! That's a fan*tastic* idea! You're . . . you're a *genius*!"

Stephen and I kept talking, and in just ten minutes a new plan was born. A better plan. An amazing plan.

Something else happened as we talked, something that made those ten minutes the best ten minutes of my life. Because during those ten minutes our friendship changed. Completely. Our friendship became a partnership—an *equal* partnership.

The new plan involved some risks—for me, and for Stephen, too. But I didn't care about the risks. And neither did Stephen.

We were in it together.

sixteen

PHASE ONE

I read on the Internet about this famous experiment that two guys did way back in 1964. They gave a test to some kids at a place called the Oak Elementary School. After the test they said the results showed that a portion of the kids were going to make fantastic progress during the school year. They called those special kids the "bloomers."

Then they gave the teachers lists of all the bloomers so that the teachers could watch those certain kids change during the year. And the kids did. The kids on the bloomer lists all made amazing progress—*real* progress.

And here's the best part: *The information was fake!* The names of the special kids, the bloomers? Those names were picked out of a hat! The only thing that wasn't fake was the *expectation* of the teachers. The teachers actually expected certain kids to make progress, and that expectation was real, and the results at the end of the year were real too. The "bloomers" all made huge progress. All because of the expectations. Because expectations can be powerful.

And by Thursday morning almost every fifth grader and all my teachers were expecting to see the new and improved Nora Rowley, girl genius.

Getting the news about me to the kids had been Stephen's job. It hadn't been hard. Philbrook Elementary School had a gossip grapevine, and Jenny Ashton was the chief grape. One whispered phone call to Jenny on Sunday night was as good as a live press conference on CNN.

Mrs. Hackney had taken care of getting the news to all my teachers. I saw the principal's memo on Mrs. Noyes's desk during homeroom. It said, "After testing and observation, Dr. Trindler has determined that Nora Rowley is a profoundly gifted child. She has apparently been keeping this to herself for quite some time."

So everybody was expecting to see a genius. Which was fine. Stephen and I were ready for that. On Thursday I was going to live up to everyone's expectations. And maybe create some new ones.

In language arts class we were studying read-ing strategies like scanning and prereading and predicting. Mrs. Noyes passed out a three-page story and we had to leave the sheets face down on our desks. Then she said, "When I tell you to begin, I want all of you to turn the sheets over, and you'll have fifteen seconds to scan the story. Then we'll turn the pages face down again and talk about predicting what the whole story might be about from what you've been able to scan. So is everyone ready? . . . Begin scanning."

Fifteen seconds later Mrs. Noyes told us to turn the sheets over, and she said, "All right, now based on what you saw in your scan, who can predict what happens in this story?"

When I raised my hand, the other kids who had their hands up pulled them down. They wanted to hear what the genius had to say.

I was the only person with a hand in the air, so Mrs. Noyes said, "Nora, what do you think this story's about?"

I took a deep breath and said, "This story's about a girl who lived during the Great Depression, and she needed to earn money so could buy a birthday present for her father. Her mother had died the year before, and she knew her dad was so sad about it that he was almost ready to give up. There were no real jobs, but the girl finds this shopkeeper who says he'll pay her ten cents every afternoon to sweep the sidewalk in front of his store. Some of her friends from school see her working and they make fun of her, but she doesn't care. She keeps working, but time is running out and she can't earn enough money. She tells her best friend and the friend tells the other kids at school. The day before her dad's birthday, all of the other kids chip in enough so she can buy the present—it's a little silver frame for her dad's favorite photograph of her mom. Her dad had been so sad, but when he sees how much his daughter loves him, his whole outlook changes and he sees that he has a lot to be glad about and so much to live for. And I think this is a story about how hard work and love and unselfishness can change a person's life."

Mrs. Noyes didn't know what to say. I had just told her exactly what happened in the story, because during that fifteen seconds I had

read all three pages. I've always been able
read that way—I sort of see a whole page as
one or two big blocks of words.

Mrs. Noyes said, "That's very good, Nora.
But was that really predicting? Didn't you just
give us a summary of the whole story?"

I nodded my head in agreement. "Yes. What
I said was more like reviewing. When you know
for certain what's already happened, you can't
actually predict about it anymore. Because
that's an epistemological impossibility. Predic-
tion has to include the idea of uncertainty—
like a theory in scientific analysis, or an
educated guess based on heuristic evidence."

Mrs. Noyes nodded slowly and said, "Um . . .
yes. Well, class, let's move on and see if we can
spot some of the clue words on the first page of
the story. Remember, we're looking for words
that will help us make some predictions."

I could feel everyone in the class staring at
me. Showing off and using some big words like
that made me feel uncomfortable. Then I took
a quick glance over at Stephen, and he had this
big, proud grin on his face. And instantly I felt
perfectly at ease.

The class moved ahead, slowly picking out clue words. Mrs. Noyes didn't call on me again during the rest of the period.

I was obnoxious all day long. In every class I found a way to put on my genius show. During art I got going with Ms. Prill about spectroscopic analysis and the different wavelengths of the primary and tertiary colors, and in social studies I had quite a lot to say about the effects of an unregulated financial market on the Great Depression.

In math class Mrs. Zhang and I had a ten-minute discussion about the best way to design a statistical analysis to try to discover the percentage of kids who would ever need to use the process of deriving the lowest common denominator once they left elementary school.

In music, when Mrs. Card said that the musical scale is made up of eight notes, I was able to point out that that's true only if you are talking about the traditional Western diatonic scale—because there are also scales like the pentatonic scale and the twelve-tone scale. And then that led naturally into a brief discussion of the use of different modal scales like the Mixolydian or the Dorian mode as the basis for musical composition.

Gym class was a challenge because it's not easy to get a conversation going with Mr. McKay. Still, I managed to offer some general comments about the structure of the inner ear and the way it affects balance and coordination.

Science was my best performance of the day. Mrs. Zhang was explaining about the speed of light. She said, "Since the sun is 93 million miles away, and since light travels at 186,000 miles per second, if the sun went out right *now*, we would still have another seven minutes of sunlight. The light traveling from the sun to the earth takes seven minutes to pass through that much space." Which was interesting and quite true. But then she said, "Nothing travels faster than light." And an idea popped into my mind.

I raised my hand, and when Mrs. Zhang nodded at me, I said, "But what about thought? If you say the word 'sun,' my thought can travel all the way across that 93 million miles to the sun and all the way back again in out one second. So since there are 420 seconds in seven minutes, doesn't that mean that thought actually travels 840 times faster than light?"

Mrs. Zhang made a strange face as she tried to get her mind around that idea. Then she shook her head. She said, "But thought isn't like light. Light is real. You can see it. You can't see thought."

I said, "Are you saying that a light wave or a light particle is more real than a thought is?"

Mrs. Zhang said, "Well . . . no, not exactly."

And I said, "So are you saying that my thought can't travel that far that fast? How about if I say 'Alpha Centauri'? See? My thought has already traveled out into space, all the way to that star and all the way back again. And light would take almost nine *years* to make a round-trip to Alpha Centauri. Unless you can prove that my thought didn't just go all the way there and back, then I'm sticking with my theory: Thought travels at least 840 times faster than light." And all around the room, kids were nodding their heads, agreeing with me.

Now, if Mrs. Zhang had said, "Nothing *material* travels faster than light," then she would have had me, and we could have talked for a while about the difference between physics and metaphysics. But she didn't take her thinking that far.

Like I said, I was obnoxious all day Thursday. A real know-it-all.

When I went to the library after school, Mrs. Byrne smiled and nodded at me when I came in, but instead of motioning me to come and talk, she quickly turned away to do some other work. Which was probably the smart thing to do. She had apparently decided to keep clear of me for a while.

Stephen came in a little after I did and sat at the opposite end of my study table.

"Well?" I whispered. "Was I horrible enough?"

He grinned at me. "You were fantastically *awful*! Every kid is talking about you. And probably all the teachers, too. I bet they're in the teacher's room right now, swapping Nora stories. It was a perfect setup—*perfect*!"

Because that was the idea. Thursday was the

etup day, the day to build up some expecta-
tions. Then we had some important events on
Friday. And the big payoff would come on
Monday. And probably Tuesday, too.

Our plan was in motion.

seventeen

HARD TEST

Friday's important events went perfectly. Stephen and I were all set for the next steps on Monday or Tuesday. But once again I learned that things don't always happen according to plan. Because Friday after school, as I sat in the library doing my outside reading, Mrs. Hackney came marching up to my table and said, "Nora? Please follow me."

The principal turned around and marched out of the media center, across the hall, and into her office. I barely had time to glance at Stephen, and he gave me a quick thumbs-up as I hurried after Mrs. Hackney. We hadn't thought this part of our plan would begin until after the weekend.

Mrs. Hackney stood behind her desk and said, "Please sit down, Nora." When I was in the chair across from her, she held up three pieces of paper and said, "I want to know something and I want to know it *right* now. *This* is your spelling test from this morning. And you got a zero on it. *This* is your math test from fourth period. And you got a zero. And *this* is your science test from two hours ago. Another zero. Three tests and you got a zero on each one. I want to know the meaning of this. We all know you are a brilliant child, Nora. And the only possible conclusion is that you have gotten these zeroes on purpose. And I *demand* to know why. Right now. Out with it—*why* did you get these zeroes?"

I had told Stephen I would be brave when our plan started to heat things up. And now I was having my hardest test of the day—the angry-grown-up-shaking-papers-in-my-face test.

Mrs. Hackney repeated the question. "Why did you get zeroes on these tests?"

I had been rehearsing my answer to that one. I said, "I got zeroes because I got all the answers wrong."

Mrs. Hackney's face bunched up until her eyes were little slits below her eyebrows. Then she found her voice and it wasn't pretty. "Don't you *dare* be smart with me, young lady! Why did you *deliberately* get every question wrong on these tests? Tell me!"

I looked her right in the eye and said, "Because all three of these tests are nothing but simple memorization, same as almost all the other tests we take. So I decided to express my opinion about this kind of testing. These tests each got the score they deserved. Zero."

This was the tricky moment. Because if Mrs. Hackney just kept getting madder and madder, I could get suspended. Or even expelled from school.

I was hoping something else would happen. And it did. Because Mrs. Hackney wasn't just a shouter, and she wasn't just some lady with an office. She was mad, but she was still a teacher—the top teacher of the whole school. She was in charge of the learning program for every grade, and I had just thrown down a challenge.

Mrs. Hackney glared at me for another few seconds, and then she sat down in her chair and began to look at the tests.

About a minute later, in a much calmer voice she said, "I see what you mean, and it's true that these tests all require students to memorize a lot of information. But knowing basic information is important. It's like the foundation. You get bored with this kind of test because you've been trying to pretend you're average—and you're not. This kind of test is fine for most of the kids. You need to be in the gifted program, Nora. In the gifted program you'd have lots of creative challenges. That's what you need. I've already talked with your mother, and I have recommended that you start that program as soon as possible. Maybe you should even skip ahead into sixth grade. Or even eighth."

I could tell Mrs. Hackney liked that skipping-grades idea. Even skipping to sixth grade would move me right out of her school. It was the instant solution: no more Nora.

But I shook my head. "What about all the other kids? I get to go and do creative and exciting things, and all the other kids get worksheets and memorization and the same old stuff, week after week. That's not fair."

Mrs. Hackney was still the principal, and she wasn't going to sit around and argue with a fifth grader.

So she stood up and said, "You may go back to the library now. I'm sorry I lost my temper, but you have upset all your teachers. A gift like yours comes with responsibilities, Nora. I want you to think about that. You have responsibilities. You may go now. But this matter is not over."

As I walked back into the library, I obeyed Mrs. Hackney: I thought about what she had just said—how a gift like mine comes with responsibilities.

Mrs. Hackney was absolutely right. I *did* have responsibilities. Except she and I had different ideas about what those responsibilities were.

And Mrs. Hackney was absolutely right about something else, too: This matter was *not* over.

eighteen

LOGIC

When I got back to my table in the library, Stephen pounced on me. "What happened? What'd she say? Are you in trouble?"

"Not too much," I said. "But she got pretty mad. And she wants to put me in the gifted program right away."

"What else?" he asked. "What about the tests and everything?"

I shook my head. "I'll tell you all about it on the bus, okay? I need to finish this reading."

That wasn't exactly true. What I really needed was time to think. Because I could see where all this was going—but I couldn't tell where it would end. The plan Stephen and I had made had sounded good when we were talking about it, and it had been kind of fun to be a show-off genius one day and then get three zeroes the next.

But something Mrs. Hackney had said really got me. She'd said, ". . . you have upset all your teachers."

And that got me thinking. If they were all upset now, how were they going to feel if we *really* got the school stirred up? Because that was probably going to happen. Our plan was to get as many kids as we could to start getting zeroes. Tests, quizzes, homework—zeroes on everything. I was just the leader, the test case.

Stephen was pretty sure that Lee, Ben, Kevin, and James would go along, and he thought he could sell the idea to his little brother and some of his friends in fourth grade, too. I thought if I explained everything just right, a bunch of the girls would join in. And that would get a whole gang of parents involved, because all of our parents were worried about grades all the time—I mean, most of our parents were already worrying about which *colleges* we would get into. So if a lot of kids started getting zeroes on everything, it would be a big deal. The story would probably get into the newspaper. And it would get onto local TV for sure, because all the school meetings were broadcast on cable. So pretty soon the whole town would know about all the bad grades.

But Stephen and I weren't planning to stop with zeroes on some tests and quizzes. Because once people started paying attention, we were going to tell everyone that we wanted all the kids in Philbrook to get zeroes on the Mastery Tests, too. If all the schools in Philbrook suddenly got rotten scores on the CMT, that would be *major* news—because if the schools get bad CMT scores, then the whole town gets a bad reputation. My mom's a Realtor, and I've heard her say that if a town gets bad scores, then fewer people want to buy houses there. Bad scores mean that the principals and the teachers get in trouble, and then the state board of education gets involved, and on and on and on.

Because those CMT scores are a *huge* deal. And since the kids are the ones who actually sit down and take the tests, the kids control the scores. That meant that the kids had all this power that they didn't even know about.

Stephen and I were ready to change all that. It was going to be like when all the teachers organized a strike and stopped working until they got paid more money. We were going to organize a kids' strike—a strike against grades and tests and pressure and bad competition.

As I sat there thinking, I could see it all happening, step by step. In three or four weeks our whole school would be turned upside down. Kids would be getting zeroes on tests. Teachers would be mad at the kids. Parents would be mad at their kids *and* the teachers *and* the principal. And the school board would be mad at everybody.

And they would all be mad at me. And at Stephen.

So that's why I needed to stop now and think.

I looked around the library.

At the next table Melanie Nissen was reading a teen romance book. She wasn't worried about her grades. She was wondering whether Roger would ever ask Susan to the big dance.

Behind me two fourth-grade boys were arguing about the best way to display their project at the science fair. They were laughing and goofing around, and they were learning, too—but they didn't even know it. And they weren't competing or thinking about grades.

Over in the corner near the magazine rack three girls were flopped on beanbag chairs, their heads close together, giggling about something. School was a fun place for them. Any pressure? Not today.

At the other end of my table Stephen was chewing on the end of his pencil and making faces at his math homework. Was Stephen desperately unhappy about school? No. Did he actually believe he was dumb—like, permanently stupid? No.

And why had Stephen gotten involved with a crazy plan that might shake up the whole town of Philbrook? Did he do it because he had a deep desire to change education in the state of Connecticut? No. He did it for me. Plus, it sounded like an adventure with a little danger and excitement.

Next fall, when it was time for all the teachers to get the kids cranked up for the CMT again, would all the kids get stressed out for a month or so? Yes, absolutely. But then the testing would be over and all the kids would get on with their lives. They would laugh and talk to their friends, they would do their homework, their teachers would teach them, they would take their tests and quizzes, and the time would go by. Then they would move on to the next grade, and the next, and the next.

Fact: I was the only kid in the whole school worrying this way about grades and tests and competition. All the other kids were being normal. And I had to face that fact, too: I was not a normal kid. I had "a gift." That's what Mrs. Hackney had called it. Some gift.

I got up and started walking toward the circulation desk. Mrs. Byrne saw me coming and she didn't look too happy about it. But I needed to talk.

I said, "Hi, Mrs. Byrne."

Mrs. Byrne smiled. "Hello, Nora. You look a little down. Hard day?"

I nodded and said, "Yeah. Did you hear anything?"

"Oh, yes—it was headline news: 'Star Student Bombs Three Tests.' Pretty dramatic." She looked into my face and said, "Is everything working out the way you wanted it to?"

"Umm . . . I don't know." And I felt like such a baby because I could feel tears at the corners of my eyes.

Mrs. Byrne pretended not to notice. She

looked down at her keyboard and then at the screen in front of her. She said, "I've been wondering about something, Nora. I hope you don't think I'm being nosy, but I'm very curious. It's a simple question: Why do you think you're so smart?"

I took a swipe at my eyes and gave a shrug. "Genetics, I guess. That's what they say if you get a supercharged mind."

Mrs. Byrne shook her head. "I don't mean *where* did the intelligence come from. I mean *why* do you think *you* have it?" She paused a second and then she said, "Think of it this way: Do you believe that things happen for a reason?"

I said, "Yes . . . at least I think that's true."

Mrs. Byrne said, "So, if things do happen for a reason, then there must be a reason that you've been given so much intelligence, right?" I nodded, and she said, "So that's what I'm asking—*why* do you think you're so smart?"

I've always felt like I could understand things instantly. Whenever a question came along, all I had to do was think, and *zip*!—an answer was right there. No busy signal. No waiting.

This question was different. I was thinking hard, but I got nothing. I said, "I don't know. I have no idea why I'm this smart. And . . . and if I don't know the answer . . . then maybe I'm not as bright as I think I am. Is that it? Is that what you mean?"

Mrs. Byrne smiled again and shook her head. "I'm not saying that. I think you're every bit as intelligent as the evidence suggests, and then some. It's just that I've met all kinds of kids with all sorts of amazing talents. And for me the big question has always been: Why? And then, usually much later, I begin to learn the answer. I get to see what they do with their lives. It's interesting, don't you think?"

I nodded.

Mrs. Byrne said, "So tell me what comes next for you, Nora. You certainly have gotten everyone's attention. What's next?"

Yesterday I would have been able to answer that question. I'd have said, "Just you wait! Stephen and me? We've got *big* plans. Watch out for lots of action and all sorts of fireworks and plenty of loud noises!"

But I didn't feel that way anymore. So I

said, "I'm not sure. There are too many variables. Everything's kind of weird now."

"Hmm." Mrs. Byrne said, "I wish I could tell you what to do, Nora. But I can't. I can tell you this, though. Of all the possible things we can do at any moment, *one* is usually better than the rest. So that's the one to look out for. All you ever have to do is the next good thing. Make sense?"

I smiled and said, "Very logical. Sounds like something a librarian would say."

That got a laugh out of her. Mrs. Byrne said, "Well, I think it's true, all the same. I know you can figure this out. And I'll be watching to see how you do."

I said, "That'll make two of us. Plus every other kid and teacher in the school."

The speaker below the clock let out a long bell tone.

I said, "See you Monday, Mrs. Byrne."

And she said, "Have a nice weekend, Nora."

I went back to my table and got my things ready for the bus ride home.

Mrs. Byrne hadn't given me any answers, and she hadn't solved any of my problems. In fact, now I had more questions than before I'd talked to her. Even so, I felt better.

Which wasn't logical.

Because the fact is, logic only works up to a certain point. Beyond that point, it takes a different kind of thinking. More like listening. And watching.

That was what I needed to do. I needed to listen and watch.

I needed to be on the lookout for that next good thing.

And if I spotted the next good thing, then would come the hard part. Because then I'd have to *do* it.

nineteen

TOO MUCH

When my mom came home late Friday afternoon, she was hugging a stack of papers.

She laid everything out on the kitchen table. "See?" she said. "Look at this, Nora. The admissions counselor over at Chelborn Academy, Mr. McAdams? Such a nice man. He was *very* happy to meet with your dad and me. And you should have seen his face when we told him about your IQ test. He thinks you might be able to begin as an *eighth* grader next fall, so we have an interview scheduled for next Tuesday, right after school—isn't that *exciting*? Look at this brochure . . . here. That's the new library. That whole building was a gift from *one* person. Lots of money at a school like Chelborn. And look at this list. These are all the colleges that Chelborn graduates got into last fall. I couldn't believe it—almost *one third* of the class went to Ivy League schools! Isn't that fantastic? And look at what Mr. McAdams gave me—it's a Chelborn Academy sticker for the back window of my car."

My mom was making plans and spinning out dreams faster than they make burgers over at Wendy's. Fact: Keeping my intelligence a secret for the past five years had been one of the best decisions of my whole life.

But now my mom and dad were trying to make up for lost time. They were going to set up a thousand hoops so their little baby-girl genius could jump through all of them, one after another.

Mom turned away to fill a pan with water and put it on the stove. Then she said, "Oh—I almost forgot. Mrs. Hackney called me at work this morning. She wants to move you into the gifted program as soon as possible. She said something about you being bored with your classes, which I can understand completely. So we're going to have a meeting about the gifted program on Monday. Isn't it wonderful? Everything is falling into place so perfectly!"

I wanted to scream. I wanted to shout, *Have you lost your mind? Did you stop for one second to think about how I might feel about all of this?*

But I didn't. That didn't seem like it would

do any good at the moment. So I just nodded and tried to smile.

The whole weekend was like that. Mom and Dad were like two little kids with a new toy—me. By Sunday afternoon they had practically planned the whole rest of my life. If they could have picked out a husband for me, and then gone shopping for my wedding dress, I think they would have.

Todd was actually happy to have the spotlight aimed completely at me. He liked the shadows—it was much safer there. But I felt bad for Ann. She liked being the center of attention and she was used to it. She had always been the smart one, the talented one, the one who was finishing high school early so she could go to a big-name college. And now annoying Nora had become the star of the family show. Ann didn't say one word to me all weekend.

Stephen tried to call me twice, once on Saturday and once on Sunday. Both times I pretended I couldn't come to the phone. That was a rotten thing to do, but I didn't know what to say to him.

After Stephen called the first time I thought, *Maybe I should call back and tell him that we need to wait a week or so before we do anything else—sort of give ourselves time to think.*

When he phoned the second time I thought, *Maybe I should tell Stephen that we have to call the whole thing off, just stop it right now and forget about our plan. Then I'll apologize to him for making such a mess of things. And then I can start trying to figure out how to apologize to all my teachers. And to Mrs. Hackney and Dr. Trindler and my mom and dad.*

And then I thought, *Maybe I should just change my name, dye my hair black, and move to Argentina.*

I went over the whole situation again and again. It was too much to think about. And I had to admit it: I was lost. I had zero facts. I was listening, and I was watching, but that next good thing was nowhere to be seen.

So I did nothing. All weekend long I lay low. I tried not to think about anything, which never works.

I knew I'd have to talk to Stephen at the bus stop on Monday morning. And I knew something would have to happen after that.

Because that's one of those completely dependable facts: Something *always* happens next.

twenty

A SHORT VACATION

Ann had earned a perfect attendance record in grades four, five, six, eight, and ten. She loved going to school. And Ann had never, never tried to stay home from school on purpose, not once—at least not during my lifetime. That's why I had been forced to turn to my big brother, Todd, to learn the fine art of malingering.

Todd pretended to be sick about once a month, usually about three days after he got a new computer game. Todd knew how to make himself throw up. He could make his face break out in red blotches. He could seem to come down with a sudden fever, and he could manufacture toilet noises that made Mom or Dad pound on the bathroom door and shout, "Todd? Todd! Are you all right in there?!" Todd was the master.

I only faked being sick when I absolutely had to, and that's how I felt on Monday morning. I couldn't deal with Stephen or Mrs. Hackney or my mom or dad or anybody. I needed to be alone.

So first I waited until Dad left for work because he's always more suspicious than Mom. Then I got myself nice and hot by stepping up and down on my desk chair about thirty times. Then I climbed into bed, pulled up the covers, and called, "Mom? Could you come in here? My stomach doesn't feel so good."

One hand on my forehead was all it took. "You feel a little feverish, too. Poor dear . . . probably one of those bugs that's going around. This is such a miserable time of year!"

A few minutes later Mom brought me a tray with a glass of Sprite and some dry toast. As she fluffed my pillows and tucked in my quilt, she said, "I've got three appointments this morning, Nora, but I'll check in by phone, okay? I called Mrs. Faris next door, and she's at home all day today. She'll come over to check on you in an hour or so—she's got a key. And I'll come home at lunchtime. If you need anything at all, you call me or your dad, all right? And you stay right here and rest."

I only nodded. I was too weak to speak.

Five minutes later a beautiful silence settled over the house. And finally I felt like I could actually think.

Except I didn't. I went downstairs to the family room and did the opposite of thinking: I turned on the TV. I flipped to The Learning Channel and toured castles in Ireland for a while, then explored the Great Barrier Reef, and then went digging for dinosaur bones in Wyoming. I was on vacation.

At about nine-thirty Mrs. Faris opened the front door and called, "Yoo-hoo, Nora, it's me, Mrs. Faris." She came into the family room, fussed around for a few minutes, and then left.

I was just beginning a submarine journey to the wreck of the *Titanic* when the phone rang. I hit the mute button on the remote, and using my sickest voice, I said, "Hello?"

It wasn't Mom. A lady said, "Hello . . . may I speak with Mr. or Mrs. Rowley?"

I've always been told never to let a caller know that I was home alone. So I said, "My dad's out in the backyard with Rolf—that's our German shepherd. May I have your name and number so my dad can call you back in a few minutes?"

There was a pause and the lady said, "Nora? Is that you?"

And then I knew that voice—it was Mrs. Hackney. I gulped and said, "Yes." And to stall for time I asked, "Who is this?"

"It's Mrs. Hackney, Nora. I need to speak with your mother."

The tone of her voice told me that this was not a social call—probably about the meeting for getting me into the gifted program.

I said, "Well, I stayed home sick today—and my dad's not really here right now. And we don't really have a dog, either. And my mom had to go out for a little bit. But she has a phone with her." Then I gave Mrs. Hackney the number.

She said, "Thank you," and she hung up before I could even say "You're welcome" or "Good-bye," or anything. Seemed pretty rude, but I didn't think about it because I went right back to my exciting undersea exploration.

Just as the first submarine was getting its remote camera into the dining room of the *Titanic*, my mom came bursting through the front door. She was halfway up the stairs to my bedroom before she heard the TV, and then in two seconds flat she was standing in front of me.

With her eyes flashing and her voice down low in the danger zone, Mom said, "Shut off the TV. Go upstairs and get on your school clothes. Now."

"But I'm sick."

Mom said, "I doubt that, but frankly, right now it doesn't matter. Get dressed. We've got to be at school in ten minutes. So move it."

"Why?"

She shook her head. "Hush. Hurry."

Three minutes later we were backing out of the driveway. I hadn't even brushed my teeth. I said, "How come we have to have a meeting about the gifted program today? What's the big rush?"

My mom kept her eyes on the road, both hands tight on the steering wheel. She shook her head. "That's not what this meeting is about. Not by a long shot. *This* meeting is about *zeroes*, Nora. Like the ones you got on those tests on Friday."

My heart started pounding. "I . . . I was going to tell you about that, Mom. That was just a crazy idea I had. But it's all over now. I'm not going to do that anymore. Honest."

My mom darted a sideways look at me, then back at the road. "Well, that's fine for you. But what about all the other kids?"

"The other kids? What are you talking about?"

Glancing at me again, Mom said, "Don't play dumb with me, Nora. *That's* never going to work again. I'm talking about the social studies quiz that Mrs. Noyes gave this morning. Mrs. Hackney just called me and said that all but two students on the whole Blue Team got zeroes on the quiz—that's *forty-two zeroes*. And because of what happened on Friday, Mrs. Hackney would like to have a little talk with you. And with me . . . and your father."

Mom was done sharing. She pressed her lips together into a thin, hard line and drove the car. It was about another two minutes to the school.

Mom hadn't given me a lot of information, but I processed all the available data.

Three seconds later I knew. I knew exactly what had happened: *Someone* had had a busy weekend.

And I knew something else, too: When Stephen had tried to call me on Saturday and Sunday, I should have talked to him.

twenty-one

REBELLION

The principal's office looked way too familiar to me. The one big difference was that today there were so many people in the room that they couldn't all fit at the round table.

One lady was sitting at Mrs. Hackney's desk. I knew who she was because I'd seen her on cable TV. It was Mrs. Tersom, the school superintendent.

Mrs. Byrne sat on a folding chair next to the principal's desk. Mrs. Drummond, the guidance counselor, was there too, and beside her was Mrs. Anderson, the school secretary. She had a notepad on her lap, ready to keep track of who said what.

Mrs. Hackney sat at her usual spot at the table. Dr. Trindler sat on her left, and then there were Mrs. Noyes and Mrs. Zhang.

My mom's eyebrows went up when she saw Stephen and his mom and dad sitting at the table. I wasn't surprised at all—I'd have been amazed *not* to see them. But then came Merton Lake and both his parents, and I had no clue why they were at the meeting.

Stephen caught my eye as I took a chair at the table, and I saw the slightest flicker of a smile. I looked away. There are times when nothing is more dangerous than a smile. This was one of those times.

About ten seconds after Mom and I sat down, my dad came rushing in, nodded a few quick hellos around the table, and took the seat next to me.

Then Mrs. Hackney said, "It's been quite a morning here at Philbrook Elementary School. Mrs. Noyes, please begin by telling us what happened during your third-period social studies class."

Mrs. Noyes nodded at Mrs. Hackney and said, "I had prepared a twelve-question quiz from the weekend reading assignment in the social studies book. We talked about the chapter, and then I passed out the quiz—it was just one page. When everyone was finished, I had the students exchange papers, take out their red pencils, and we began discussing the answers.

There was a lot of laughing as we corrected the quiz, so I began walking around the room. And I saw that almost every student had written a nonsense answer to every question."

Mrs. Hackney said, "A nonsense answer?"

"Yes," said Mrs. Noyes. "For example, on the question, 'Who was the president of the United States at the start of the Great Depression?,' students wrote answers like, 'Donald Duck' or 'Elvis' or 'my uncle Lenny'—very silly. And wrong."

Mrs. Hackney said, "And what grade did most of your students get on this quiz?"

Mrs. Noyes glanced at me before she answered. "Zero. All but two of them got a zero. And then during fourth period, when the other half of the Blue Team has social studies, I warned the class before the quiz that there was to be no funny business. But when the quizzes were graded, it was the same thing—all zeroes, except for two of the students who didn't participate in the . . . silliness."

I'd have bet anything that one of those two kids was Merton Lake. But it wasn't important at the moment.

Mrs. Hackney said, "Who wants to start explaining this?"

Stephen and I both said "I do" at the same moment, but I was the one who kept on talking. "It's all my fault, Mrs. Hackney. I got this idea that if I got some zeroes on tests, and then if we talked some of the other kids into getting some zeroes, we could get people to notice how everybody is so crazy about grades and test scores all the time, and how that's kind of a problem. So this whole thing was my fault."

Stephen shook his head and said, "That was my idea, the part about getting zeroes. And then we worked on the plan some more together. But that part was my idea, remember?"

At that moment I wished Stephen could have been a little less honest—because then he would have seen that I wasn't trying to steal the credit for his idea. I was trying to keep us both from getting run out of town by an angry mob of teachers and parents.

But Stephen wasn't clever that way, and there wasn't a sneaky bone in his body. Which is one of the things I've always liked best about him.

So I said, "Okay, yes. That part was your idea, but *I* was the one who was putting the idea into action. I was the one who started things off by getting some zeroes last Friday, and then we didn't talk this weekend, and I guess you must have called a bunch of kids, right? And that's why everyone else got zeroes today. But it's still really my fault. And I'm sorry. And now it's all over."

Mrs. Hackney said, "I wish it were that simple, Nora. But it's not. First, there's the matter of this handbill that Stephen was trying to pass out in the halls today." She passed sheets of paper to her left and right. I stared at my copy as Mrs. Hackney read the words out loud.

CALLING ALL KIDS!!
Tired of stupid tests???
Tired of fighting for grades????
Do you hate those Mastery Tests?????
Then join the rebellion!!!!!
ENLIST TODAY!!!!!
HOW?
SIMPLE!!
GET A ZERO ON YOUR NEXT TEST!!!
LET'S SHOW EVERYBODY
THAT WE CAN THINK FOR
OURSELVES!!!!!!!!!
QUESTIONS? ASK STEPHEN CURTIS.

Mrs. Hackney looked at Stephen and then around the room. "Rebellion," she said, "is not something we need or want at Philbrook Elementary School."

I was stunned. I couldn't believe Stephen had done something so bold. And he'd put his *name* on that thing! And then he'd gotten all but two of the kids on our team to actually *do* it, too! Stephen must have talked on the phone the whole weekend.

Mrs. Hackney continued, "And then there's the matter of Stephen and Merton's fight."

Mr. Lake raised his hand and said, "I don't accept that. It was *not* a fight!" He pointed at Stephen. "*That* child attacked my son, and Merton was forced to defend himself. And don't forget that Merton is one of the two students who did *not* go along with this . . . this conspiracy!"

I'd never seen Merton's dad before, but I was guessing he was a lawyer.

Mrs. Curtis glared at him and said, "Stephen has never *attacked* anyone in his life!"

Mrs. Hackney said, "Please. Let's stay focused here. There *was* a shoving match in front of the school this morning, and it looked like trouble o the teacher who was out there on bus duty. And Mrs. Byrne had to pull *both* boys apart to stop it. Isn't that right?"

Mrs. Byrne nodded. "Yes. It wasn't exactly a fight, but it was certainly headed that way. It was a definite skirmish."

I almost smiled at that. Leave it to Mrs. Byrne to find the perfect word—*skirmish*.

Mrs. Hackney said, "Very well. I'd like to summarize our situation. We have two students who have admitted that they organized and encouraged rebellious behavior. And we have two boys who were nearly fighting. But our most serious problem is that half of the fifth-grade class decided to treat two quizzes as if they did not matter at all. They treated their schoolwork like it was a big joke." Mrs. Hackney glanced around the table. Then she looked right at me and said, "A disobedient attitude has been set loose in our school. And we have got to *stop* it. Now."

The lady sitting at Mrs. Hackney's desk stood up. Everybody turned to look at her and she said, "I'm Julia Tersom, Superintendent of Schools. When I spoke with Mrs. Hackney an

hour ago, I advised her to isolate the ⌐
Team students from the other children in t⌐
school. That's why they've all been in the
library for the past forty-five minutes. The
nurse and the custodian are acting as emer-
gency substitutes so their regular teachers
could be here at this meeting."

Mrs. Tersom paused.

There's a special way that presidents and
mayors stand and tilt their heads and hold
their hands when they give important
speeches. That's how Mrs. Tersom looked.

She swung her eyes slowly across her audience and said, "About a year ago we had a
problem with vandalism at the junior high
school. Lockers were damaged; mirrors in the
washrooms were broken; walls were written
on, and books were destroyed. And I'm sorry
to report that it took more than eight months
to get that vandalism completely stopped.
Why did it take so long? It's very simple:
because the principal of that school did not
jump on that problem soon enough—or *hard*
enough. Our situation today is not quite as
serious as vandalism, but it's not so different

er. If the children who got zeroes on those uizzes go to lunch forty minutes from now and start laughing and bragging about what they've done, this defiant attitude could easily spread to the rest of the school. And that must not happen. That is why we have to handle this problem forcefully . . . and immediately. Every student in the Philbrook schools must understand that tests and grades are serious business. Every student in our schools must always try to do his or her best to earn excellent scores. That's what education in Philbrook is all about—excellence. And right now those students in the library are confused about that. So we've got to solve this problem in the next thirty minutes. Mrs. Hackney?"

Mrs. Hackney smiled briefly and nodded. "Thank you, Mrs. Tersom. What we're going to do is have a meeting with the whole Blue Team, right now, just across the hall in the media center. We are going to stay focused on the facts, and we are going to point out the mistakes that have been made. We are going to make it clear that this kind of behavior *cannot* and *will not* be tolerated ever again. And to emphasize the seriousness of this matter, Tersom and I have decided that Nora Row and Stephen Curtis are suspended from schoc for two weeks—effective immediately."

My first thought was for my mom and dad. Mom gasped and then sat there like a statue, her back straight and stiff, and I could see the beginning of a tear at the corner of her eye. Dad's face showed pure disbelief. I felt terrible for them.

And then I saw Stephen, sitting there trying to get his mind around what that meant— "suspended from school for two weeks." His face was pale, and both his mom and dad were looking right at me. There was no doubt in anybody's mind: I was the cause of this whole mess. And that's how I felt too.

I imagined what would happen at the big team meeting. There would be a long lecture with Mrs. Hackney shaking her finger a lot. And Mrs. Tersom would be frowning at our friends and threatening to kick everyone else out of school—just like they were suspending Stephen and me. And of course, Merton Lake would be sitting there the whole time with a

little smile on his face. Awful. And there
nothing I could do about it.

Fact: Once a plan starts to collapse, it comes
crashing down fast. All you can do is try to
jump out of the way. And sometimes you
can't.

Mrs. Hackney was about to say something
else when Mrs. Byrne raised her hand. The
principal said, "Yes, Mrs. Byrne?"

Mrs. Byrne stood up and smoothed the front
of her skirt. "Mrs. Hackney, I need to say
something. I do not agree with this punishment." Her voice wasn't loud, but it was
strong. "I think that the motives of Nora and
Stephen should be taken into account here.
The things they did may have been naive, and
they have certainly caused some problems for
Mrs. Noyes and Mrs. Zhang and our fellow
teachers. But these two weren't simply trying
to stir up trouble. And what they've been
doing has absolutely *nothing* in common with
vandalism, Mrs. Tersom. Vandalism is mindless
and destructive, and what Nora and Stephen
have been doing is anything but that."

Mrs. Hackney stood up and leaned forward

with both her hands on the table. "That's qu
enough, Mrs. Byrne. This is neither the tim
nor the place for personal opinions."

But Mrs. Tersom held up a hand. "It's all right, Mrs. Hackney. We have nothing to hide here. Our school district has always been a place for free and open discussion. So please continue, Mrs. Byrne."

Mrs. Byrne nodded at the superintendent and said, "Thank you. As I was saying, these are good kids, and their motives were good. These students were simply trying to get everyone to look more closely at some of the negative side effects of testing and grading. The teachers at this school, and at every other school in our town, have raised the same kind of concerns. And teachers all across Connecticut have pointed out that this focus on test scores is unhealthy—especially the CMT scores. Nora has experienced these issues firsthand, and she's intelligent enough to have noticed the problems, and she and Stephen have been brave enough to try to do something about it— braver than some of the rest of us have been. So I want to go on record here. I am flatly osed to these suspensions. And I think that many of the other teachers in our schools—and perhaps a good number of the people in the town of Philbrook—would agree with me."

When Mrs. Byrne finished, Einstein would have loved it. It was like that timeless moment before The Big Bang.

Then the universe began to explode.

There was a short burst of applause as Mrs. Zhang and Mrs. Noyes got up from the table and walked over to stand beside Mrs. Byrne. They were "fellow teachers" like Mrs. Byrne had mentioned, and teachers stick together.

My mom stopped holding her breath. My dad nodded at Mrs. Byrne and said, "That's right—maybe Nora's on to something here," which got him a gentle "Shush!" from my mom.

Mrs. Curtis patted Stephen's arm, and Stephen began to get some color back in his face. Then my mom and Mrs. Curtis started talking back and forth above my head. Stephen's dad took out a handkerchief and blew his nose, and then wiped his forehead—which was the wrong order, if you think about it.

Merton's mom had one eyebrow lifted she whispered something in her husband's e Merton sat there with a twerpy grin on his mug and he tried to catch my eye, but I ignored him.

Mrs. Hackney tried to keep her face muscles under control, and in the middle of all the noise and chatter she kept saying, "Let's stay focused, people!"

The superintendent looked around and kept her lips pulled back into a tight smile, but her eyes told the real story. I could see her imagining what might happen if this issue broke loose and started bouncing all over town.

The school secretary had given up trying to take notes, and when she started talking with Mrs. Drummond, words and phrases floated across the table. "Really? . . . Oh, yes. Because on Monday it was only . . . and when she told me that . . . noo! You're *kidding*! . . . Yes, I heard that too!"

Dr. Trindler just smiled and tapped his fingertips together. The psychologist was enjoying himself.

And me? I was trying to see everything at once.

en I looked at Mrs. Byrne. She was in her
air again, her hands folded on her lap. We
exchanged a look, only for a second. A lot was
said during that glance. It was not a kid-to-
teacher moment. It was person to person.

Finally Mrs. Hackney pushed her voice up
an octave and said, "Come to order, please.
Everyone! Please, quiet down!" And when the
room was quiet, she said, "Thank you. Now, I
have an idea or two, but perhaps our superintendent should give us her thoughts first."

Mrs. Tersom kept her smile locked in place,
but I could tell she had no clue what to do.
Again her eyes gave her away. I could see her
problem—everyone could: If she took too
strong a stand, she might have a *real* rebellion
on her hands. And if she took too weak a
stand, then she would lose some of her author-
ity.

Mrs. Tersom said, "Well, I . . . I really think
that, all things considered, we shouldn't try to
handle this at the district level. This is a local
school issue, and since you're the principal,
Mrs. Hackney, I think we should hear your
ideas first."

It was another Einstein moment, time and space suspended, all eyes on Mrs. Hackney's face.

Everyone could see what was happening. Two powerful, intelligent women were each scared to take the next step. And I felt bad for both of them. After all, I was the one who had gotten everyone into this mess in the first place. I wished I could help them.

Then something began happening. Something new.

I've always been the lightbulb girl. Thoughts would come blasting out of nowhere, like a lightning bolt on a sunny afternoon—BOOM!—and I'd have a new idea.

This was different. An idea was definitely coming, but softly. It was like I was looking at a broad, green lawn, and then there was a passing cloud or a shift in the wind, and every blade of grass snapped to attention, sharp and crisp.

And there across the lawn I could see the footsteps of an idea, a simple path, and I could see it had always been there. And the path was for me.

All I had to do was the next good thing.

I raised my hand.

Mrs. Hackney had never been happier to call on someone. "Yes, Nora?"

I don't know why I stood up before I started talking, but I did. I said, "If it's all right with you, Mrs. Hackney, I'd like to talk to the whole Blue Team. I think . . . I think I need to say something . . . to everyone. And then, whatever you and Mrs. Tersom decide to do about punishments and everything, that'll be okay with me."

And instantly Stephen stood up and said, "Me too."

There we were again, equal partners.

Mrs. Hackney looked from Stephen to me, and then turned to look at Mrs. Tersom. Mrs. Tersom turned to look at me, and then she looked back at Mrs. Hackney. And then Mrs. Hackney looked at me again and said, "That sounds like a reasonable request. I think we should all walk across the hall to the library right now."

It must have felt like a reasonable request to everyone, because the whole room seemed to heave a sigh of relief.

As people started getting up and m[...]
toward the door of the office, my dad lea[...]
my way and whispered, "I sure hope you kno[...]
what you're doing."

I whispered back, "Me too."

twenty-two

THE NEXT GOOD THING

It took a while to get everyone settled in the media center. The chairs and tables were pushed aside and the kids sat on the floor in the middle of the room. All the grown-ups and teachers sat on chairs at the edges and in the back.

It didn't feel like an assembly or a weekly meeting. There was no squirming, no whispering, no giggling. There wasn't even any smiling. It felt like a funeral—*my* funeral.

Mrs. Hackney stood in front of the main desk and waited until the last grown-ups were seated. I stood beside her and Stephen was next to me. My mom and dad were sitting off to the left. They seemed a million miles away, and I thought how nice it would feel to be sitting there between them again.

It was hard to breathe. I knew what I wanted to say, but I wasn't sure how to begin. Or how to end. Then I thought, *What about*

Stephen? What's he going to say? I mean, [he]
who could make that kind of a handout co[uld]
do anything! What if he raises one fist an[d]
shouts, "Hey, everyone! Kids rule! Let's get this
rebellion going!" and then he starts running
around the library, ripping books off the shelves
and breaking the furniture? Or . . . or what if
Mrs. Hackney changes her mind all of a sud-
den, and she stands there and points at us and
says, "Nora and Stephen have been wicked,
wicked children, and I've decided that they
shall both be expelled from school forever! Out!
Get out of here, both of you!"

Imagination can be torture, so I was glad when Mrs. Hackney started talking.

She looked around the room slowly as she spoke. "We are here this morning because some serious mistakes have been made. I think all of you know what I'm talking about. Nora Rowley has asked if she could speak to the whole Blue Team, and I've given her permission. Stephen Curtis has something to say too." Then she looked at me. "Nora?"

No long speech, no extra time to think. A few quick sentences and now it was all up to me.

looked out over those faces and I froze. I
gulped. I opened my mouth. I tried to begin,
but nothing came out.

So Stephen said, "Nora and I started talking
about something last week, and that's what she
wants to tell you about."

I nodded, and I gulped again, and then I
said, "Yes. It was about grades. I've been worried about grades for a long time. I think a lot
of kids do that, but I wasn't just worried about
getting good grades or bad grades. I was worried about grades themselves, about the whole
idea of grades. Because grades and test scores
can make kids feel like winners or losers. And I
didn't like that. Because I saw some kids start
thinking they were dumb after we all took the
Mastery Tests last year. And they weren't
dumb, not at all. So I wanted to do something
about that. And I guess it wasn't so smart to
think that I could change everything by myself,
or even with Stephen's help. Or that everything could change quickly. Because that's not
how things happen. But I felt like I had to do
something . . . anything. And then Stephen and
I got this idea about getting zeroes, but that

made it look like we thought school was a j
or something. And it's not a joke. We don.
think that. We just wanted everybody to look
at the numbers and the letters and the test
scores and really think about them. But things
went too far, and then everybody got upset,
and I don't want that. I know school's important, and it's important to do good work, and I
think almost every kid does—good work, I
mean. And the teachers do, too. And I didn't
understand how a lot of teachers feel sort of
the same way I do about testing and grades. So
we have to do things together. To make things
better. And that's all I wanted to say. That I'm
sorry about the trouble. Because there are
other ways to make things better."

Stephen nodded and said, "Yeah, I'm sorry
too. And especially for that stuff about rebellion. I know why it happened, though—like,
why I made that flyer and everything. Because
it was exciting. I mean, all of a sudden I felt
like my grades didn't have this huge power
over me. And I guess I got carried away. Even
so, I learned a lot. And I'm not going to be
afraid of tests and grades anymore, not like I

. But I'm sorry about the trouble, like Nora
..d."

I waited for more, but Stephen was done.

I didn't see, but I think it was my dad who
started the clapping. And then everyone
clapped a little, even Mrs. Tersom. It was
pretty embarrassing.

But Mrs. Hackney held her hands up and it
got quiet right away. She said, "I know we have
all learned some important lessons today, and I
know each of us will remember how important
it is to always do our best work. And now I'd
like the team teachers to take all the students
to their homerooms until you are dismissed for
lunch."

And that was it. We were done. No more
talk of being suspended, no threats, no shouting,
no finger shaking. I followed Mrs. Hackney's
orders and started moving toward my homeroom teacher. It seemed too good to be true.

It was. From about fifteen feet away the
principal called, "Nora—please ask your mom
and dad to join me back in my office for few
minutes. And you, too."

A minute later we were face-to-face with

Mrs. Hackney again. And then Dr. Tr[...] came in and sat down.

Mrs. Hackney said, "I'm glad the morning has ended as calmly as it has, but there's another matter to discuss. We need to resolve Nora's placement. Dr. Trindler and I feel that she needs to be in the gifted program."

My mom nodded and said, "We agree completely. We're going to have some independent testing done, and Nora's going to take a placement test at Chelborn Academy next week. But the gifted program should be fine until we see where she really belongs."

Dr. Trindler said, "Excellent. Most students currently in the program take two to six gifted periods each week, but in Nora's case we feel that except for homeroom, gym, art, and music, she should be in the special-classes pod all day."

Someone so close to getting kicked out of school probably should have kept her mouth shut, but I couldn't. I didn't even raise my hand or ask if it was all right if I talked. I just blurted it out. "I don't want to be in the gifted program. I like my teachers, and I like my s, and I want to stay where I am."

r. Trindler smiled and said, "We can all nderstand your reluctance, Nora. Change is always a little scary. But you can't help being who you are. You are extremely intelligent. You just are. You are so far above average that the normal classes move too slowly for you."

I shook my head. "But if I finish my work or if I already understand what the teacher's talking about, then I can just think about something else. I've always had plenty to think about. I'll run math problems in my head. I'll think about the poems I've got memorized. Or I can get out a book and read. I want to stay in the normal classes because I like normal kids. I don't want special treatment, and I don't want teachers who are always trying to push me ahead."

Mrs. Hackney wasn't trying to butt in and neither were my mom and dad. This was between me and Dr. Trindler.

He said, "But think of it this way, Nora. How will you reach your full potential if you don't accept new challenges?"

"I'm not trying to be a smart aleck, but

please, think about that," I said. "Am I r
trying to get away from new challenges?
you think that trying to be normal after what
happened this last week won't be a new challenge for me? And that stuff about working up
to my full potential—who gets to say what my
full potential is? An IQ test? Shouldn't *I* have
something to say about what I want to accomplish? What if what I really want is to be normal? What if being normal is my big goal in
life? Is there anything wrong with that? To be
happy and read books and hang out with my
friends and play soccer and listen to music? To
grow up and get a job and read the newspapers
and vote in elections and maybe get married
someday? Would that be so terrible? I know
that I'm different, and I hope I'll always be
smart. But I don't want to get pushed ahead so
that I'm always trying to do what someone else
thinks a person with my intelligence ought to
be doing. I want to use *my* intelligence the way
I want to use it. And right now I want to be a
normal kid."

While I was talking, it was like the words
poured into my mind and out of my mouth

milk from a pitcher. I had never given a
ech like that before.

And when I stopped no one said anything.

So I said, "May I go to my homeroom now?
It's almost lunchtime and I don't want to be
late. It's pizza today."

"Yes, Nora, you may go."

And my favorite part is that it wasn't Mrs.
Hackney who said that.

It was my mom.

Lunchtime was a little weird, and my afternoon classes were strange too. There was a lot
of whispering and I felt kids looking at me
almost every second. It must have been sort of
like the way a movie star feels at the grocery
store. But I just tried to mind my own business
and have a regular day. I tried to be normal.

The rest of the day had two best parts.

The first was when I went to see Mrs. Byrne
right before I got on the late bus. I had been
playing soccer in the gym, so I was hot and
sweaty and a little out of breath. I was cutting
it close because I hoped the library would be
empty. And it was. Mrs. Byrne was alone, sitting

at her screen at the front desk. I think she
me coming, but she didn't look up until I w
right in front of her.

She smiled and said, "Big day?"

I smiled back. "Huge. Did you hear anything?"

"Oh, yes. More headline news in the teach-
ers' room: STUDENT SAVES HER OWN SKIN,
THEN WINS FOLLOW-UP DEBATE. Very dramatic.
I'm proud of you."

I blushed. "It wasn't so special."

Mrs. Byrne shook her head. "That's where
you're wrong. It was. Everything you've
done has been quite special and remarkable
and wonderful."

I started to talk, but she said, "And don't say
that you couldn't have done it without my
help. There's an old saying: Nothing can stop
an idea whose time has come. And this time is
your time, Nora. Now, hurry up—run and
catch your bus."

I said, "Well, thanks all the same, because you
did help me—tons," and I started to go. Then I
turned back and said, "Mrs. Byrne, what college
has the best courses in library science?"

he said, "There are a number of fine pro-
ams—why do you ask?"

"You know," I said. "In case I want to reach
my full potential."

Mrs. Byrne laughed and shooed me out the
door.

But really, I wasn't kidding.

The other best thing was after the bus ride.
Ben got off at the corner too, but his house was
in the other direction. So it was just me and
Stephen walking along the road.

He didn't say anything until we got to my
driveway. He kicked at the gravel with the toe
of his sneaker. "What you said in the library
about kids thinking they were dumb after the
test last year? That was me, wasn't it?"

I nodded. "Yeah. It was you."

He looked at my face and then at the
ground. "So all this was kind of about me?"

"Yeah. Kind of . . . but it was about me, too."

"Well, yeah," he said. "You mean about you
being smart and everything, right?"

"Yeah," I said. "All that."

He smiled and said, "Maybe it would've
been kind of fun to be suspended a couple
weeks, d'y'think?"

"I don't think so," I said. "Too boring. A lot of stuff happens at school."

"Yeah," Stephen said. "A *lot*!"

I couldn't think of anything else to say. Neither could Stephen.

He said, "So I'll see you tomorrow, okay?"

"Yeah," I said. "See you tomorrow."

And then I went up my driveway and he walked toward his house.

That three minutes with Stephen wasn't so much if you only look at the events, like a scientist would. Because, really, what happened? Hardly anything. Stephen hadn't tried to do something like carry my book bag. He hadn't looked into my eyes and said, "Nora, you're my best friend in the whole world." And we hadn't had a deep discussion about school or tests or grades.

We just spent a little time together at the end of the day. Stephen talked to me like a friend. Like I was a normal person. Just me, Nora.

At that moment nothing could have made me happier.

And that's a fact.